ay and
ha guns drawn, hammers
bac squeezing the triggers. He
smiled, relishing the moment.

That was when a pistol cracked—a single shot barely heard above the pandemonium. The fat lawman recoiled as if slapped, his brow knitting as a red rivulet trickled from a neat little hole above his heart. His pistols sagged, as did he, his mouth working soundlessly. His body collapsed heavily into the dust.

Fargo peered through the gunsmoke to see the small form of Wes holding his derringer. The boy had just killed a man, but his calm made him seem frighteningly old. He looked at Fargo, speaking with almost no emotion.

"My first lawman."

**"Mr. Fargo! Behind you!"**

Fargo spun. The sheriff was ten feet away...
...ed him dead to rights. Both guns...
...k, pudgy lifeless...
...ed...

# THE TRAILSMAN

#214

# TEXAS HELLION

by

## Jon Sharpe

Ⓢ

A SIGNET BOOK

SIGNET
Published by New American Library, a division of
Penguin Putnam Inc., 375 Hudson Street,
New York, New York 10014, U.S.A.
Penguin Books Ltd, 27 Wrights Lane,
London W8 5TZ, England
Penguin Books Australia Ltd,
Ringwood, Victoria, Australia
Penguin Books Canada Ltd, 10 Alcorn Avenue,
Toronto, Ontario, Canada M4V 3B2
Penguin Books (N.Z.) Ltd, 182–190 Wairau Road,
Auckland 10, New Zealand

Penguin Books Ltd, Registered Offices:
Harmondsworth, Middlesex, England

First published by Signet, an imprint of New American Library, a division of
Penguin Putnam Inc.

First Printing, September 1999
10  9  8  7  6  5  4  3  2  1

The first chapter of this book originally appeared in *Apache Wells,*
the two hundred thirteenth volume in this series.

 REGISTERED TRADEMARK—MARCA REGISTRADA

Printed in the United States of America

# The Trailsman

Beginnings . . . they bend the tree and they mark the man. Skye Fargo was born when he was eighteen. Terror was his midwife, vengeance his first cry. Killing spawned Skye Fargo, ruthless, cold-blooded murder. Out of the acrid smoke of gunpowder still hanging in the air, he rose, cried out a promise never forgotten.

The Trailsman they began to call him all across the West: searcher, scout, hunter, the man who could see where others only looked, his skills for hire but not his soul, the man who lived each day to the fullest, yet trailed each tomorrow. Skye Fargo, the Trailsman, and the seeker who could take the wildness of a land and the wanting of a woman and make them his own.

*1861—Texas, where the men are wild,*
*the women are willing, and killers*
*come in all shapes and sizes. . . .*

# 1

It was hot enough to fry an egg on a flat rock.

Texas was baking under the worst summer heat in years, and Skye Fargo had no choice but to pass through the inferno on his way west. His buckskins were plastered to his muscular frame. Beads of sweat dotted his bronzed brow, above his piercing lake blue eyes. Removing his hat, he ran a hand through his slick hair, then pulled the hat low again, the brim slanted to shield the upper half of his face from the relentless sun. His throat was as parched as the countryside but he would find no relief anytime soon. He'd used the last of the water in his water skin two days ago, and it was very likely the next water hole would be as dry as the dusty ground over which his pinto stallion plodded.

The Ovaro was having a hard time of it. For almost a week the horse had baked as if in an oven. A week of one hundred-plus temperatures, of sweltering every minute of every day, of scant forage. The stallion needed rest and plenty of sweet grass, but most of all it needed to quench its burning thirst.

"Sorry, big fella," Fargo muttered, then licked his sore, cracked lips.

No wind stirred. No animals were abroad. Even the lizards had taken shelter for fear of being roasted alive. It was the middle of the afternoon, the worst part of the day, and Fargo hadn't seen another living thing since midmorning. So the flitting of a shadow on his right drew his gaze skyward to a large dark bird winging westward.

A crow, Fargo thought, blinking sweat from his eyes. But no, the thing was larger than any crow, and had a leathery red head. It was a buzzard, hurrying to join half a dozen others circling ahead.

Fargo didn't rate it worth much interest. Earlier that day he'd come across the carcass of a doe picked clean by scavengers, and he figured the buzzards were about to feast on another wild creature the hot spell had claimed. That is, until he saw a partial hoofprint, and then a black bulk on the ground ahead, shimmering in the heat under the pinwheeling birds.

Straightening, Fargo clucked to the pinto. Or tried to. He had to wet his mouth and lips twice before he could make a sound. The weary stallion broke into a brisk walk, the saddle creaking as Fargo shifted to rest a hand on the Colt nested in a holster on his hip. In his right boot, snug in an ankle sheath, was a deadly Arkansas toothpick, and from the saddle scabbard jutted the stock of his trusted Henry. A man on the frontier had to be well armed or risk forfeiting his life.

Tracks, which Fargo could now see clearly, told the story. Someone had ridden the dead horse into the ground. Deliberately, from the look of things. The hapless animal had staggered the last hundred feet, sheer will forcing it on even after its sinews had given out. Not once had the rider stopped or slowed. Now the horse was on its side, a roost for a dozen buzzards that had already arrived. One probed its beak into an eye socket. Another had ripped open the horse's belly and was tugging at an intestine.

Fargo rode right up to the carrion eaters, heedless of their hissing protest. They didn't like having their meal interrupted and were loath to leave. Many glared, a few snapped at him, and finally, with a loud flapping of strong wings, they abandoned their meal. Ungainly at first, they rose sluggishly, several feathers spiraling in their wake. One passed so close to Fargo's face, he could have snatched it out of the air. But he sat still until the last of the scavengers were far overhead.

Dismounting, Fargo received several mild surprises. First, the dead horse wasn't a horse at all, but rather a pony, black with white socks and a white blaze. The tongue, or what was left of it, protruded from distended lips. Second, the rider had left the saddle on, including the saddlebags. Third, a neat hole between the pony's ears showed that although the rider had been careless enough to let it collapse, he'd been decent enough to put the poor animal out of its misery.

Boot prints pointed westward. Fargo leaned down to better study them, then recoiled as if he had been slapped. They were small tracks, typical of a boy or girl of ten or so. Sitting up, he shielded his eyes with a hand, hoping for some sign of the youngster, but he hoped in vain. In the distance were only empty, rolling hills.

"What's a child doing alone in this godforsaken country?" Fargo asked aloud. Saloon rowdies liked to say that Texas was no place for greenhorns or amateurs. It was also no place for children to be wandering by their lonesome. Especially in the remote stretches, where fierce beasts and savage men lay in wait for the unwary. The region thereabouts was infested with bears, mountain lions, and occasional jaguars. To say nothing of Comanches.

Climbing down, Fargo stripped off the saddlebags and opened them. In one pouch was a spare homespun shirt and pants, both in need of mending and washing. In the other were seven small pieces of quartz, a broken folding knife, the single blade a rusted stub, a seashell like those found along the Gulf of Mexico, a rabbit's foot attached to a string, and—of all things—a turtle shell.

His brow knit in thought, Fargo closed the flap. The bay's rider was a boy, that much was obvious. Fargo strapped the saddlebags on behind his own, then forked leather and headed out, paralleling the scuffs and scrapes left by the youngster's boots. The length of the boy's stride told Fargo he had started off across the plain rapidly enough, but was soon shuffling along like a drunk, withered by the heat.

Fargo fully expected to stumble on the boy's prone form before too long. Judging by the condition the bay was in, he guessed it had given out about the middle of the morning. Which meant the boy had been afoot for five hours. Five whole hours under the burning sun. It would be a miracle if the youngster still breathed.

Minutes dragged past and nobody was to be seen. Now and again Fargo rose in the stirrups but didn't spot any sign of life. The tracks led him steadily on, and within an hour he was drawing rein at the base of the hills. Normally a lush and green land, the drought had sucked all the vigor and vitality from the foliage, leaving the landscape a dull, dusty brown.

The boy's tracks had gone up into the trees, his steps livelier, probably in anticipation of finding water.

Eager for the same reason, Fargo nudged the Ovaro on. Once among the big pines and oaks, welcome shade washed over him. Removing his red bandanna, he mopped his brow and neck, then wrung it out. As he rounded a pine, the pinto suddenly nickered and halted of its own accord.

"Reach for the pearly gates, mister, or you'll be passing through them before you know it!"

Dumbfounded, Skye Fargo sat there with the bandanna in his hands, too stupefied to do as he'd been commanded. Barring his way was a pint-sized bundle of rawhide and whipcord in dirty clothes and a battered brown hat a size too big. The boy couldn't be more than ten or eleven years old, just as Fargo had reckoned. Cherub cheeks and a button nose lent him an innocent look belied by the derringer he held rock-steady in either hand.

"Wax plugging your ears?"

"What the hell?" Fargo declared, resisting an urge to laugh. "What do you think you're doing, boy? Put down those parlor guns before someone gets hurt."

The left-hand derringer cracked, the lead whizzing near

Fargo's ear. Tendrils of smoke curled from the stubby barrel as the boy wagged it.

"That's the only warning you get. Climb down, and be right quick about it. I'm borrowing your pinto."

Fargo had half a mind to jump down, wrest the derringers away, and throw the boy over his knee. "Listen, son," he said. "I saw your pony. I know what happened. How about if I give you a ride to the next town and—"

The youngster didn't let Fargo finish. Taking a step, he extended the other derringer and thumbed back the hammer. "There are more pills in here for what ails you."

"And what might that be?"

"The worst case of the stupids I ever did see. You must be part Yankee, mister, to be so dumb. Now quit trying my patience, and slide off!"

Something in the boy's pale blue eyes warned Fargo not to take him lightly. There was a certain coldness, an icy calm rare even in adults. Swinging his leg over the saddle horn, Fargo eased to the ground. "Don't do anything you'll regret."

"What's to regret about killing somebody?" the boy said so matter-of-factly, it was startling. "I wouldn't regret crushing a bug, would I?"

"Bugs and people aren't the same," Fargo said, to keep the pint-sized hard case talking.

His brow furrowing, the boy remarked, "I wonder. My pa is always quoting Scripture to us, going on about the Commandments and such. Do you know the one that says, 'Thou shalt not kill'?"

"I've heard of it," Fargo said dryly.

"It doesn't mention people. It says we're not to kill at all. But then my pa sends me out every day to kill critters for the supper pot. Does that make any kind of sense?"

Before Fargo could answer, the boy motioned, indicating he should move further to the right. Elevating his arms to give the impression he wouldn't cause any trouble, Fargo complied. "Does your father know where you are?"

"No. I ran away. I had to. Got to find my cousin. And as ma always says, blood is thicker than water."

Fargo tensed his leg muscles as the youngster sidled toward the pinto. "Your cousin?"

"Never mind. It's none of your affair." The boy wedged the left-hand derringer under his belt. "I've wasted enough time jabbering. Back up a little more."

"You'd steal a man's horse and leave him stranded?" Fargo stalled. "Didn't any of that Scripture-reading your father did sink in?"

"Nice try, mister. But if I won't feel guilt over blowing out your wick, I sure as blazes won't feel none over stealing your horse."

The boy was clever beyond his years. Fargo made a mental note not to treat him like a typical ten-year-old. "Why don't you let me take you where you need to go? We can ride double."

About to reach for the saddle horn, the boy hesitated. "If I thought I could trust you, I might just do that. But if there's one thing I've learned in life, it's never to trust adults. A lying pack of coyotes, the whole bunch of you."

"Does that include your father?"

Anger flushed the youth's cheeks crimson. "Don't you ever insult him again! My pa never told a lie in his life. He's a Bible-thumper, mister. A preacher."

Fargo's puzzlement grew. How was it possible this cold-blooded sprout could be the son of a minister? Something didn't quite add up, and he sorely desired to learn more. "I'm serious about my offer. I'll help you get where you need to go, and I give you my word I won't cause you any trouble along the way."

"How do I know you're not talking with two tongues, as the Injuns like to say?"

"You'll just have to trust me."

The boy leaned against the saddle. "I'd like to be able to believe you, mister. I surely would. But too much is at

**6**

stake." Shifting, he rose on his toes but couldn't quite rise high enough to mount.

Fargo tried one last time. "What can it hurt? I'll even let you hold on to my Colt, if that will make you feel any safer."

"Thanks for reminding me. I plumb forgot." The boy pointed the derringer again. "Shuck that hardware of yours. Nice and slow, if you don't mind. You're a friendly cuss and all, but I can't take chances."

Sighing, Fargo undid the buckle. "Suit yourself. But you're making a mistake you might regret."

The boy shrugged. "I've made them before, I'll make them again."

"Mind telling me your name?"

"John Wesley—" The boy caught himself. "Who I am isn't important. Most folks just call me Wes. What's your handle?"

Fargo told him.

"Well, Mr. Fargo, don't hold this against me. If we should meet up when it's all over and I have the time, I'll explain. But now I've got to light a shuck." Again Wes rose onto his toes to try and snag the saddle horn but the stallion was a lot larger than his pony had been. "Darn it all!"

Fargo spun, whipping the holster at the boy. His intention was to swat the derringer aside and rattle the youngster so badly, disarming him would be easy. But Wes was quicker than Fargo expected, incredibly quick for one so young. The boy, pivoting, ducked under the belt, and made as if to shoot.

"Now why did you go and do that? See? You're just like all the rest." Wes's pale eyes were as flinty as quartz. "No more fooling around. Drop the damn belt and take ten steps back, or I'll drop you, so help me God."

It was aggravating to be bossed around by someone who wasn't old enough to shave, but Fargo did as he was instructed. An inner instinct warned him that Wes would put a slug into him without batting an eye. "I'll be coming after my horse," he said.

"You do that." The boy was unperturbed. "I'll leave it at

a stable once I don't have any more use for it." Hiking a leg, he managed to snag a stirrup. Then, by clinging to the pommel and the cantle, he was able to pull himself high enough to fork leather. "Be seeing you." With a cheery wave, he slapped his legs against the pinto and was gone.

Fargo half hoped the Ovaro would buck the boy off. It had a temperamental streak and was fussy about who could straddle it. But the stallion hastened on up the hill with no more than a low nicker.

There was a moment, just before Wes reined around a thicket and was gone, when Fargo could have scooped up the Colt and shot him. But he wouldn't—he couldn't—put a slug into a child. Reclaiming the gunbelt, he buckled it on and trudged after the stallion.

Despite the shade, Fargo was soon sweating as much as he had out on the plain. Within a mile he had developed a cramp in his left calf which wouldn't go away even after he flexed his leg and massaged the tight muscles.

Wes had ridden due west, ever deeper into the burning hills. Up one slope and down another, Fargo hiked for the next three hours. He pulled his buckskin shirt out and let it hang over his gunbelt. He tied the bandanna around his forehead, just under his hat, to soak up perspiration that might trickle into his eyes.

His feet were aching like the devil when Fargo plodded from the woods into a field and paused to tighten the bandanna. The sight that met his eyes when he looked up was enough to cause him to blurt, "I'll be damned!"

On the far side reared several buildings. Old and dilapidated, coated with dust and grime, they had been constructed from planks long since warped and split by the elements. Fargo thought it must be an abandoned homestead until he saw hogs in a pen attached to the decrepit barn and heard a rooster crow.

Wading through the high, dry grass, Fargo licked his cracked lips in anticipation of a cool glass of water. Texans were hospitable by nature, and more than willing to lend a helping hand to those in need. He might be able to talk the homesteader into lending him a horse. As tired as the Ovaro was, overtaking it wouldn't take long.

The tracks led toward the house. Fargo assumed the boy was long gone and scanned the hills beyond but they were empty of life. Except for half a dozen chickens and the hogs, the same could be said of the homestead. No one was out and about. The front door was shut, and burlap flaps covered the windows. He wondered if maybe the owner had gone abroad somewhere.

Stopping beside the porch, Fargo hollered, "Anyone home? I'd be grateful for a drink!"

There was no reply. Other than the soughing of the breeze and the clucking of the poultry, the place was as quiet as a tomb. Fargo stepped onto the porch, removed his hat, and rapped on the door twice. The sound resounded dully, as it would on a hollow log. "Anyone here?" he called out.

Stepping to a window, Fargo tried to peer in but the burlap was nailed tight. Which was strange, given how hot it was. Most people would leave the burlap off to take advantage of any wind. He tried a third time.

"I mean you no harm! If you're here, show yourself!"

Fargo decided he was wasting his breath. He tried the wooden latch but the door was locked. Leaving the porch, he circled around the house, seeking another way in. Most homesteaders kept pitchers of water handy on their kitchen counters, and he had no qualms about helping himself.

Then he spotted something even better; a well.

A crudely built ring of waist-high stones was flanked by two stout posts supporting the handle, a wound rope, and a battered bucket. Hurrying over, Fargo cranked the bucket downward into murky depths. He had no idea how deep the well was, but the scent of moisture was strong enough to make him dizzy. At last a faint splash heralded success, and he swiftly spun the handle in the opposite direction.

Fargo heard water slosh over the side. When the full bucket rose into view, he beamed with relish. Leaning over, he gripped it in both hands and raised it to his mouth to drink to his heart's content.

"Hold it right there, stranger."

At the rear of the house a scruffy man had materialized, a scarecrow in clothes as run-down as the house itself. A straw hat roosted on a head that reminded Fargo of the buzzard's. Big eyes, a hooked nose, and a pointed chin completed the portrait. Bony thumbs were hooked in the pockets of his dirty pants.

"I called out," Fargo said, "but no one answered."

"And that gives you the right to help yourself?"

"I'm as dry as a desert," Fargo said, annoyed by the man's attitude. "I didn't think anyone would mind if I took a drink."

"You thought wrong!"

This statement came from the front of the house, from someone other than the scarecrow. Fargo glanced around and discovered a second homesteader, a bulky ox in similarly ratty clothes. But this one held a shotgun in his brawny, calloused hands. "Not very hospitable, are you?" Fargo said lightly.

Snickering, the scarecrow ambled forward. From the corner of his mouth dangled a short piece of straw. "Our home. Our well. Our water. We have the right to do as we damn well please. If we don't care to share, there's nothin' you can do about it."

Fargo looked at the water, so cool, so inviting, then at the shotgun. At that range it would blow him in half. Reluctantly, he set the bucket down. "I suppose it would be useless to ask for some grub?"

"About as useless as tits on a bull," the scarecrow said. Halting, he nodded at the human ox. "That there is my brother, Orville. I'm Theo Mosely. We bought this spread from Old Man Tyler about four years ago and we've been bustin' our backs tryin' to make do ever since. We have a few head of cattle yonder, some horses and hogs, and what have you."

Fargo had no interest in their personal history. Incensed at being denied, he debated whether to slap leather and treat himself at gunpoint.

Theo had gone on. "Dry as it's been, mister, we need every drop of water for us and for our stock. You'll just have to get by until you come to Webber Creek, about ten miles further on. Providin' it hasn't dried up, like it often does this time of year."

Fargo remembered Wes. "Did you let the boy who stopped by have any? Or did you send him on his way without so much as a sip?"

The brothers exchanged looks. "Which boy is that?" Orville responded. "You're the first to pay us a visit in pretty near two months. We're off the beaten path, you might say. The nearest town is Hender's Gap, two full days to the northwest."

Clearly imprinted in the dust at Fargo's feet were the Ovaro's tracks and a few of Wes's. Fargo also noted a small spot where the ground had been damp a short while ago but was now almost dry. Someone—and it was unlikely to have been the Moselys—had spilled a little of their precious water. "He stole my horse."

Both men laughed wickedly. Orville sauntered up, a thick thumb curled around the shotgun's twin hammers. "A full-growed feller like you let a sprout swipe his animal out from under him? What did he do? Pounce on you and wrestle you to the ground?" They laughed louder.

Holding his resentment in check, Fargo gave the bucket a last, lingering glance. "I was hoping he'd stopped here. My mistake." He moved around the well, contriving to keep it between Orville and him. As casually as he could, he rested his right hand on his revolver. "I'd better get to that creek while I have some light left."

The pair were taken aback by Fargo's abrupt departure. Out of the corner of an eye he saw Orville arch bushy eyebrows at Theo, who shook his head.

"Good luck findin' your stallion," the scarecrow said good-naturedly.

"Be careful that sprout doesn't beat you to a pulp," Orville threw in.

Fargo walked on past the barn. He pretended to be interested in the chickens, but they were an excuse to keep his head turned so he could watch the Moselys. Orville was itching to cut loose with that cannon, he could just tell. Theo had to gesture twice to persuade his brother to lower it.

Another field separated the homestead from a strip of trees. Once he was shrouded by vegetation, Fargo hunkered and pondered. They were playing him for a fool. Maybe they figured that with all the tracks made by them and their stock, no one could pick out individual prints left by Wes and the Ovaro. And they were right, as far as it went. Most people lacked the skill. But Fargo wasn't like most others. He was one of the best trackers alive. Years ago he'd lived among the Sioux and learned the craft from a warrior who could track a chipmunk over rocky ground.

The Moselys had made another mistake. Theo had wished Fargo luck finding the stallion, but Fargo had only mentioned having his "horse" stolen. So how was it Theo knew what kind it was, unless the brothers had seen the Ovaro? Added proof was that no tracks led from the yard. The Moselys must have Wes and the pinto, both.

Fargo intended to sneak back for a closer look. The question, though, was when? Common sense urged him to wait for dark so it would be safer. But sunset was over an hour off yet, and by then something might happen to the boy, if it hadn't already.

"Hell," Fargo muttered. Angling to the right, he looped to the side of the field nearest the hog pen. Four sows were rooting their snouts in the muck and filth, another three dozed in the sun.

Theo and Orville were gone. Into the house, Fargo hoped. Doubled over in a crouch, he cat-footed through the grass, parting the stems with his hands so the grass wouldn't rustle loudly and give him away. As he stepped into the open, the biggest hog swung toward him and squealed loud enough to rouse the dead. Fargo immediately flattened and waited for the brothers to investigate. After a couple of minutes elapsed and neither did, he heaved to his feet and dashed to a side door in the barn.

Within, a horse whinnied. A hoof stamped. Fargo lifted the latch and the door creaked inward. The great double doors at the front were closed, the interior shrouded in deep gloom. Slipping inside, he pressed his back to the wall and let his eyes adjust.

There were six stalls on either side. Over half were occupied. Edging to the center aisle, he checked the first one on the right. A mare pricked her ears and sniffed. He glided to the next, which held a cow heavy with calf. She was contentedly chewing hay, her tail swishing at flies. Fargo moved on. He took another two steps when the metallic rasp of a gun hammer being pulled back stiffened his spine.

"You should have kept going, mister!" Orville Mosely bellowed.

At that, the barn thundered to the blast of the shotgun.

# 2

The bellow gave Skye Fargo an instant in which to react, and he made the most of it by diving onto his stomach. Above him, the buckshot tore into a stall, showering bits of wood all over him and the straw-littered ground. One barrel spent, one barrel to go.

Fargo heard Orville swear as he moved to the right, rolling over and over to make himself harder to hit. Ponderous footsteps came closer, and just as Fargo rolled into an empty stall the shotgun discharged a second time. Earth erupted like a volcano, spewing clods and dust. He felt a stinging sensation in his left leg, but looking down, he saw it was only a nick.

Rising, Fargo palmed the Colt and swiveled. Between two boards, he glimpsed Orville's hulking shape retreat into the gloom. Surging upright, Fargo banged off two swift shots, eliciting a yelp as Mosely disappeared behind bales of hay.

Without delay Fargo launched himself into the aisle, crossing it in three long bounds and sliding into another empty stall. Silence descended, silence which didn't last long. The horses commenced to nervously prance and nicker, while the cow let out with a long-drawn bellow. Outside, the chickens were squawking as if a hawk were in their midst, and in the vicinity of the house a dog barked.

Fargo quickly replaced the spent cartridges and inserted a

sixth under the hammer. A hint of movement by the hay was sufficient to let him know Orville had also reloaded. Lying flat, he removed his hat and poked an eye past the end of the stall.

The big lummox thrust his head above the bales, his gaze glued to the stall Fargo had just vacated. Grinning slyly, Orville dashed toward the stalls Fargo was hiding among, his back to them as he moved down the row until he was directly across from the one he thought Fargo was still in. It gave him a clear shot, but unfortunately for him Fargo was no longer there. Confused, he looked right and left.

That was when Fargo rose and jammed his Colt against the man's back. "Let go of the shotgun or die."

Orville didn't quibble. "Whatever you say, mister," he responded, and obeyed. "Just don't squeeze that trigger. It'd be murder, pure and simple."

"What do you call what you almost did to me?" Fargo searched for sign of the other brother.

"I figured you were fixing to steal one of our horses. And in Texas a person can protect their property as they see fit."

"I only want my stallion, and the boy."

The ox's broad shoulders rose and dipped in a shrug. "I don't know what you're talkin' about. We've already made it plain that you're the first visitor we've had in a month of Sundays."

Fargo was tired of being taken for a jackass. Pumping his arm, he brought the revolver crashing down into Orville's thick skull. The blow would crumple most men but Orville merely staggered on legs gone as soft as mush. "One last time. What did you do with the kid and my horse?"

Orville didn't know when to stop bluffing. "You can pound on me all you want but I still don't have—"

Fargo struck three times in swift succession, pistol-whipping Mosely as a lawman would a rowdy drunk. Orville fell to his knees and tried to twist to get at him, but Fargo slammed the barrel across a temple.

15

Sprawling onto his hands and elbows, Orville yelled, "I've had enough! Stop!"

"Not until you tell me where they are." Fargo kicked him in the ribs, then raised the Colt to bash the crown of his head.

"Please! I'll talk! I'll talk! Just don't hit me again!" The fear in Orville's beady eyes was genuine. Fingers splayed protectively over his face, he whimpered like a stricken puppy. "Your horse is in the first stall on the right."

"Show me."

Orville was slow in rising. Scarlet drops flecked his face and neck and he had a nasty gash above one ear. "I hurt something awful," he complained.

"I don't give a damn." Fargo pushed him. "Move."

Sulking, Orville lumbered toward the front of the barn. He licked drops from his mouth and pressed a sleeve to the gash. "You're a mean one, mister. Snake-mean through and through."

"Think so?" Fargo smashed the Colt against his jaw and Orville dropped like a sack of potatoes. Stepping around the still figure, Fargo smiled on seeing the pinto right where Mosely had claimed. His saddle was on a nearby rack with a lot of other tack, most worn beyond repair. The Ovaro nuzzled him as he patted its neck and scratched behind its ears.

All the while, Fargo glanced from the great doors to the side door and back again, sure Theo would rush to his brother's aid. But there were no outcries, no sign at all the other Mosely was still around. A groan brought Fargo to Orville's side. "Now show me where the boy is. And for your sake, he'd better be alive."

"You about busted my chin," the big man angrily declared, rubbing it. "Keep wallopin' me and I won't be in any shape to show you anything."

"The boy," Fargo said pointedly.

"Damn, you're a persistent cuss." Growling like a wild beast, Orville painfully rose and tottered toward the great doors. He threw a shoulder against them and they parted on hinges long neglected, squeaking noisily. Only an hour of daylight remained, and the barn's lengthening shadows were spreading and mingling, totally eclipsing the house.

"Where is he?" Fargo demanded.

Orville jabbed a thick finger at a ground-floor window. "Locked in a room. He's tied up, but we never laid a hand on him, as much as Theodore wanted to."

"How's that?"

"The brat is a real scrapper. He put up a hell of a fight. Damn near put a slug into Theo, then bit a chunk out of his leg. Theo was all for brainin' him, but we always wait and see if any kin comes callin'."

*Always?* Fargo prodded Orville to hurry him along. "So this is how you make ends meet? By stealing and murdering?"

The ox clamped his lips together.

"The marshal in Hender's Gap will be interested in what you've been up to," Fargo mentioned. "I'll turn you over to him after we're through here."

Unaccountably, Orville chortled, then smothered his mirth by placing a hand over his mouth.

"What's tickled your funny bone?"

"Hender's Gap ain't much of a town, stranger. They don't have much in the way of law, and what they do have is real partial to us local boys."

Since they were approaching the porch, Fargo didn't give the statement much thought. Staying close behind Orville in case Theo opened fire, he climbed the stairs. The front door was ajar.

Orville opened it all the way and tramped indoors, his bulk filling the narrow hallway. "It's the third room on the left."

A peculiar odor assailed Fargo, an odor both foul and sickly sweet, an odor as familiar as every buffalo carcass he had ever come across, yet it took him a few seconds to recognize it for what it was. When he did, he drew up short,

**17**

gouging the Colt against Mosely. "Where's that smell coming from?"

"Ma's bedroom." Orville gestured at the next door on the right.

"Open it."

The stench grew worse, so nauseating Fargo placed a forearm over his nose and mouth and breathed shallow. Motioning for Orville to back away, he peeked into the bedroom and couldn't credit his own eyes.

A bed, primly made but covered with dust, was in one corner. In another sat a dresser well past its prime. But it was the rocking chair in the center of the room that shocked Fargo. Or, rather, the remains of the person *in* the rocking chair. For slumped in it was the body of a woman long dead, dressed in a plain yellow dress and a green bonnet. Her flesh had shriveled, her eyes had sunk into their sockets, her fingers were gnarled talons gripping the arms of the rocker as if for support. "That's your mother?"

"Ain't her bonnet pretty?"

"She's dead."

Orville tittered. "Shucks, any yack can see that. Ma died over a year ago, of consumption. Theo and me couldn't stand the idea of worms and maggots and such gnawin' on her, so we dressed her in her best clothes and set her there."

"Why didn't you build her a coffin?"

"Neither of us know how."

Fargo stared at him.

"Ma was the smart one in our family. Thanks to her we were able to get by even when times were hard. But after she died we couldn't make a go of it. We had to sell off a lot of our cattle. Then Theo had a brainstorm."

"Robbing people is a brainstorm?"

"Every little bit helps. Take that pinto of yours. Down in Houston or San Antonio, it'll fetch a good price. Enough to keep us going for a long while. And sooner or later someone else is bound to come along with another fine animal."

"What do you do to the owners?"

Orville clamped his mouth shut again. But he'd revealed enough for Fargo to guess the truth. The brothers were as vile a pair of cutthroats as ever lived, preying on hapless travelers and squirreling away their ill-gotten gains so they could go on living in a dump no one else would pay two bits for. "Show me the boy."

Muffled sounds broke out the moment Orville pushed the door wide. Lying on a bed, trussed like a goat for the slaughter, was young Wes. A gag had been stuffed into his mouth and he was blindfolded. Another rope had been wrapped around his neck and tied to the headboard so he couldn't move more than a foot in any direction.

"See? He's fine."

Cold rage seethed through Fargo. Yes, the youngster was alive and well but he wouldn't have been for long. "Turn around," he snapped.

"Aw. You're not fixin' to wallop me again, are you?" Orville slowly rotated. "I wouldn't have let my brother hurt the boy. Honest. I like kids! I was one myself, once. We'd have kept him locked in here, sort of like a pet, and I would feed him and give him water when he needed some. That's not so terrible, is it?"

"You don't know how much of an idiot you really are," Fargo said furiously, and brought the Colt crashing down with almost all his might, folding Mosely like an accordion. Fargo didn't waste another second in springing to the bed and prying at the knots digging into Wes's throat. The boy flinched and would have pulled back but Fargo said, "It's me. Be still and I'll have you out of here in two shakes of a lamb's tail."

Wes uttered a string of words distorted by the gag.

"Here," Fargo said, yanking it out.

"Where are they? I heard you talking to the dumb one. Give me a gun! No one does this to me! No one!"

"Simmer down or you'll bust a gut," Fargo quipped, loosening the blindfold. Rope still bound the boy's wrists and legs, but when Wes caught sight of Orville in the hallway, he started to struggle to get off the bed to wreak vengeance. "Enough!" Fargo pinned him with one hand. "From now on you do as I say or I'll leave you here to fend for yourself."

"You wouldn't!"

Of course Fargo was bluffing, but he didn't want the boy to know that, so he rose and made for the doorway. "I'll let the law in Hender's Gap know where you are."

"Wait!" For the first time uncertainty and anxiety were mirrored in Wes's pale eyes. "I know when I'm licked. I give you my word I'll do as you say until we're out of this mess. Then it's every man for himself."

Fargo had to smile at the boy's use of the word "man." "That'll do for now." He finished untying Wes and offered to help him off the bed, but Wes pushed his arm away and hopped down with the agility of a cat. "Have you seen any sign of the other brother?" Fargo needed to know. "Theo?"

"The ugly one? No. Last I saw, he tied me up and walked off laughing." The youngster held his hands out. "I'm asking you again for a gun. I don't care what kind. I don't feel right without one."

"I only have one." Fargo checked the hallway before venturing out. Theo might be anywhere, lying in ambush.

"We can't leave without the derringers," Wes said. "They must be in the house and we have to find them. They're not mine."

"Tell your father you lost them."

"Lose a gun?" Wes cocked his head and regarded Fargo as if he were loco. "Where I come from, we're taught to shoot almost as soon as we're taught to walk. Ever since I can recollect, I've toted a gun of some kind. Mostly it was my pa's old rifle." He paused. "Those derringers are my uncle's. I snuck them from his cabin and he won't take kindly to me losing them. But I had it to do. For my cousin's sake."

Another mysterious reference to his cousin. Fargo had a slew of questions but they had to wait until the two of them were safe. Drawing the Colt, he stalked toward the front door. Nothing moved in the yard. Stopping to verify the porch was deserted, he glanced over a shoulder. "When I say so, run like hell for the—"

The boy was gone.

"Wes? Where are you?" Fargo swore and hurried back down the hall. The bedroom was empty. So were the next two rooms. At the end was a kitchen. An iron stove splotched with rust and a large lopsided table was all it boasted. On the table was a pile of dirty dishes and filthy pots, along with mold-encrusted silverware and a couple of big knives.

*Big knives?* Fargo saw the back door was open and ran to it. To the south, a handful of cattle grazed. An outhouse was to the north, and close by stood a large shed.

Fargo bent low and flew past the jamb. He made it to the shed without incident and wrenched on the door. Suddenly, something shot toward him from out of the shadows, and he automatically brought up the pistol. It was only a bird, a sparrow he had spooked. Huge holes in the ramshackle roof explained how it had got there.

No Wes, however.

Spinning, Fargo scoured the property. Where could the boy have gone? After the derringers? After Theodore Mosely? A sudden screech was Fargo's answer. He sprinted toward the barn where a commotion had broken out. Horses were nickering. Someone wailed stridently. A shot sounded, and then Theo staggered back through the great doors, a hand clasped to his left thigh, a smoking Remington in the other. The hilt of a kitchen knife jutted from his leg.

Halting, Fargo took aim.

"You damned brat!" Theo screamed into the barn. "I'll make wolf meat of you if it's the last thing I do!"

*"Mosely!"* Fargo shouted. When the scarecrow pivoted, the Colt was squarely trained on his sternum. But that didn't stop him from bringing the Remington to bear, trying to gun Fargo down. The Colt banged first. Punched backward by

the impact, Theo teetered, recovered, and stabbed the Remington at Fargo as if it were a knife instead of a gun.

"You won't kill me! I won't let you!"

At the Colt's next retort, Theo's limbs jerked like a marionette under the control of a deranged puppeteer, performing a bizarre dance. Then he melted, oozing to the grass like so much candle wax, the Remington hanging upside down from his trigger finger.

"It can't end like this!" he gasped.

But it did.

As Fargo confirmed that his shot had been fatal, the pint-sized hellion ambled from the barn. "Were you trying to get yourself killed? You should have waited for me."

Wes walked up to the dead man and without a qualm, yanked out the kitchen knife as if it were the most natural thing in the world to do, then wiped the blade on Theo's shirt. "I need those derringers and I figured he might have them. I figured wrong."

"You can always buy your uncle new ones."

The boy snorted. "Dog my cats! Why didn't I think of that?" His sarcasm was masterly. Becoming serious, he said, "No, I can't. Our family is dirt poor. My pa doesn't hardly make enough to keep us in clothes, which is why he's studying to be a lawyer."

"How about if I staked you the money?"

The wariness of a cornered wildcat crept into the youngster's expression. "Why would you do that for someone you've just met? Thanks, but no thanks. We were raised never to be beholden to anyone. And to solve our own problems." He marched toward the house. "I won't rest until I find the two Sharps."

The boy wasn't referring to the type of rifle Fargo once favored, but to the derringers. Sharps and Company manufactured a variety of firearms, and while not as famed for their short guns as their long arms, they sold reliable weapons depended on by thousands.

Fargo made no attempt to stop him. He had a lot to do

himself. In the barn, hanging on a peg, was a coil of rope which he needed. Jogging to the house, he rolled Orville over and bound the man's wrists. As he was securing the last knot, Orville stirred and groaned.

"Land sakes. What hit me? Who—?" Orville's eyes opened and he regarded Fargo in bewilderment. "Do I know you, mister?" The fact his wrists were tied sank in. Struggling, he sat up. "Now I remember, you mangy son of a bitch! You can't treat us like this. I'm going to bust your head wide open!"

The Colt blossomed in Fargo's hand. "Like hell you will."

Orville was a simpleton, but he wasn't stupid. "You're holdin' all the cards for now. What's next?"

"Help me bury your brother," Fargo said. He knew it was a mistake the instant the words were out of his mouth but he couldn't cram them back in. He barely set himself before Orville reared up off the floor like a grizzly gone amok and slammed into him with the force of a battering ram.

"No! No! It can't be!"

Even with his hands tied Orville was dangerous. His immense strength coupled with his berserk wrath rendered him as hard to stop as a rampaging bull buffalo. Short of putting a bullet in his brain or heart, little else would slow him down. Fargo found that out when he clubbed Orville twice on the side of the head, only provoking a roar worthy of a silver-tip.

Momentum propelled them out onto the porch. Fargo tried to slip to one side but arms as thick as tree trunks pinned him against Orville's barrel chest. In the next second, he was driven into a post, jarring every bone in his body to the marrow. The world spun, his gut churned. Iron fingers clawed at his gun hand, seeking to strip him of the Colt.

"Die! Die!" Orville ranted.

Fargo's vision steadied, and in front of him floated a mask of sheer and total hatred. Tearing his gun hand free, he shoved the revolver into Orville's ribs but was prevented from firing when Orville's elbows smashed into his knuckles, numbing his fingers. As Fargo locked his knees to gain leverage, he was wrenched to the left and hurled like so much chaff. The earth rushed up to meet him.

"Die! Die!"

Dazed, Fargo saw a boot arc toward his body. He couldn't avoid it, and the pain it caused was exquisite. He tumbled, losing the Colt, then surged halfway up and slid his hand into his boot for the Arkansas toothpick.

Flailing his bound arms as if they were a club, Orville waded toward Fargo in a frenzy. Again and again he pounded Fargo down, smashing him on the head, the shoulders, the back, beating and beating until Fargo's ears were ringing and his cheek was split.

"Die! Die!"

An old-timer once told Fargo there was no stopping a man who refused to be stopped, and now Fargo learned the wisdom of that saying firsthand. He attempted to rise, to resist, to fight back, but he was like a leaf in a gale, powerless against Orville's onslaught.

"Why won't you die, damn you?"

The pounding stopped. Fargo looked up and saw Orville stomp over to a pile of wood. Stooping, the riled ox probed about and came up holding a rusty ax, which he slashed back and forth in savage glee. Then he faced Fargo and charged, his maniacal grin widening.

Desperately twisting, Fargo felt air swish by his neck as the ax sank into the sod with a *thud*. He uncoiled, producing the toothpick, but he couldn't match his adversary's greater reach. It was either retreat, or be decapitated or maimed.

Orville's eyes were dilated, his nostrils flared. In the grip of unshakable bloodlust, he shrieked, *"Diiieeeeeee!"*

Fargo was so intent on the ax he neglected to glance behind him, and his heel slipped on an unseen round object as he fell. In a twinkling Orville Mosely towered above him, the ax hoisted for a fatal stroke. But then, to Fargo's surprise, Orville froze.

"You!"

"Me," said the voice of someone old beyond his years. "I don't want to kill you, mister, if I can help it. You talked your brother out of hurting me so I owe you."

"Go away, boy."

A derringer cracked and a small hole appeared high on Orville's shoulder. He recoiled but didn't release the handle.

It gave Fargo the chance to shift just enough to see Wes holding the twin parlor guns. He flipped quickly to the right, a fraction of a second ahead of the downward sweeping ax. As he rose, his arm flashed and the Arkansas toothpick leaped like lightning from his hand to Mosely's throat, imbedding itself to the hilt. Orville halted, flung the ax down, and clutched at the knife. A sharp pull was all it took to remove it, but doing so turned his neck into a crimson geyser. Gurgling and futilely striving to stem the flow, he pitched to his knees.

Wes showed no more emotion than if he were watching grass grow. He tucked the derringers under his brown belt, "Now we're even, mister. You saved my hide, I've saved yours. I'll take one of their horses and be on my way. Adios."

"Hold on," Fargo called after him, but the boy ignored him. Orville was doubled over, weakening fast, the front of his shirt and pants soaked in blood, a pool forming around his legs. Fargo threw the ax well out of reach, then retrieved the Colt.

"I—I—" Orville struggled to talk but the effort was too costly. Curling onto his side, he placed his palm over the ragged cavity in his jugular.

Fargo had another decision to make. Should he stop Wes from leaving and force the boy to take them to Wes's parents, or should he let the youngster wander off to God-knew-where on some mysterious quest?

"I hope—" Orville rasped harshly. "I hope you rot in hell for what you've done. You should have let my brother and me be."

People, Fargo mused, had an amazing knack for blaming

25

others for their own shortcomings. He took a seat on the steps to await the end. It would be fifteen minutes or more before Wes saddled up and left, he thought. But in half that amount of time, hooves drummed and out of the barn trotted the mare. The boy didn't bother to wave and was off like a shot, lashing the mare as he'd no doubt lashed the pony out on the plain when he rode it to its death.

Mosely was clawing at the earth as if digging his own grave. Then his legs started trembling, and convulsing, he expired with a fluttering groan.

Fargo rose. The two brothers needed burying, but digging a hole big enough would take the better part of an hour. And that would give Wes too much of a head start. Some days, nothing ever went right. "Damn it," Fargo declared, and raced to get the Ovaro.

# 3

Skye Fargo caught up with the boy half an hour later. He had to push the Ovaro to do so, and for his effort received a stony glare. Wes wasn't pleased to see him but never said a word. Not long afterward, darkness claimed the land. For a while Fargo thought the youngster planned to ride the whole night through. When they came to Webber Creek, though, Wes finally halted.

To call it a creek was stretching the truth. A hand-width wide and a finger-length deep, it meandered down the center of an otherwise dry bed. In spots the flow narrowed even more, but it was steady.

Fargo let the stallion drink before he did. Wes had no such consideration for the mare. Plunking himself on his belly, the boy guzzled greedily, slopping water all over his chin and shirt.

"Does riding horses to death come naturally to you?" Fargo asked.

Wes raised his dripping face. "What's that supposed to mean?"

"A man should always think of his mount first, himself second. Our lives depend on our animals. Out here, a good one is worth its weight in gold."

Wes glowered. "Why are all grown-ups the same? My folks are always lecturing me about what's right and what's wrong, too. Ma in particular. Don't do this, don't do that.

Chew with my mouth shut, hold the door for ladies, no cussing or spitting. It's enough to give a guy fits." He sat up. "Why did you come after me, anyhow? I didn't ask you to."

"I think you need some help."

"And you're willing to stick your neck out on my account? What are you? A Bible-thumper, like my pa?"

"Not hardly." Fargo began to strip the pinto. Even he couldn't say why he made it a habit to help people in need. Butting into the affairs of others was dangerous. But he could no more turn his back on someone than he could stop breathing. He spread out his bedroll close to the bank and set his saddle on top to serve as a pillow. "I have something of yours," he said, then tossed over the saddlebags he had stripped off the dead pony.

Wes didn't have a bedroll of his own. He'd laid out his saddle blanket and was seated cross-legged, wiping his derringers clean with the bottom of his shirt. "You saved my stuff for me?"

"No one should be without their lucky rabbit's foot," Fargo joked.

"I'm obliged. I truly am."

Fargo opened his own saddlebags and took out two pieces of pemmican. Some frontiersmen preferred plain jerky but he liked the taste of pemmican more. Especially when berries or chokecherries were added to the mixture of fat and meat—usually buffalo that had been pounded into fine particles. Wes was fixed on him like a starving wolf on a fawn, so Fargo flipped a piece onto the other blanket. "When was the last time you ate?"

"I don't rightly recollect." The boy scooped it up and crammed half in his mouth in one bite. He chewed noisily, smacking his lips with relish. "This is downright delicious. How come my ma never made us any? Where'd you get it?"

"From a Shoshone woman." Fargo didn't elaborate. He had stopped at one of their villages for the night and been treated to typical Shoshone hospitality. Her name had been Spring Flower, although Wildcat would be more accurate.

She'd bitten and clawed him so much during their lovemaking, he was covered with deep scratches the next morning.

Wes stopped chewing. "This is Injun food?"

"Food is food to an empty stomach."

"Maybe so. And I'm too hungry right now to pass it up. But if I weren't, I wouldn't touch it. In my family, we fight shy of heathens. They bear the mark of Cain and should be shunned by all God-fearing folk."

To Fargo, that last comment sounded like a quote. From the boy's father? Or someone else? "The mark of Cain?"

"Haven't you read Scripture? How Cain slew Abel and God put a mark on him to set him apart from all the rest? We're to have nothing to do with those who bear it."

Fargo never had much tolerance for bigots. "Indians are more like us than you might think. There are good ones and bad ones. I learned much of what I know about tracking and hunting from them." Hating people because of the color of their skin was as ridiculous as disliking them because of the clothes they wore. It wasn't what was on the outside that counted, it was what was inside.

"The only Injun I've ever met is Old Joe. He comes around begging for table scraps now and then." Wes treated himself to another bite. " 'Course, I've heard a lot of stories about the Comanches. How they butcher folks in their sleep, and abuse women. Knowing Indians isn't something I'd brag about."

"You have a lot to learn about life, boy," Fargo said, and was surprised when Wes laughed merrily.

"That's what my pa tells me all the time. He thinks I'm too uppity. That no good will come of having a mind of my own, as he calls it."

"Maybe your father has a point."

Wes had a ready argument. "Why is it that when grown-ups do as they want, it's all right, but when somebody my age does it, we're being contrary? I may be young but there are some things I won't stand for. Doing wrong by my kin is one of them."

Fargo didn't let the opportunity go to waste. "Which brings us back to your cousin. Tell me what the trouble is."

The boy's features clouded. "Susie Dixon is the sweetest girl you'd ever meet. When I was six, and my pa and ma were off to New Orleans, Susie nursed me when I had the fever. Now her damned drunk of a father has sold her, and I figure to fetch her back."

Fargo wasn't as shocked as an Easterner would be. In some states, selling people was as common as selling merchandise in a store. Slavery was rife in the South and elsewhere, and it wasn't uncommon in poorer parts of the country for white girls and boys to be sold off like cattle. Often, it was done to pay off a debt, and the "sale" would only be temporary, until the child had worked off the money owed by their parents.

"Does her father know what you're up to?"

"My uncle's head is stuck so far down the bottle, he wouldn't notice if the world came to an end."

"Is this the same uncle who owns the derringers?"

"You ask too blamed many questions." Wes lowered himself onto his side, turning so his back was to Fargo. "I'll be getting an early start. If you oversleep, don't hold it against me if I'm not here when you wake up. Good night."

Fargo sat until midnight, reflecting on the boy's strange mix of politeness and sass. He had his faults but he also had virtues, not the least of which was a keen sense of loyalty and honor, of sticking by his kin come what may. He had to admit Wes had a point about adults. In grown-ups a strong will was praised, while in children it was frowned on. Two standards were in effect; one for everyone over sixteen, another for those under it.

Fargo turned in, lying on his back with his hands folded behind his head. It had been an eventful day, and with John Wesley to watch over, those ahead promised more of the same. He listened to the wavering yip of a coyote, the plaintive cry lulling him to sleep. His last thought was that he might be letting himself in for a lot of grief, and he should light a shuck for Arizona while he still could.

Hardly any time at all seemed to go by, when suddenly a noise snapped Fargo's eyes open. Sparrows were making a ruckus in the bushes. To the east, a pink band decorated the horizon.

Stretching, Fargo rolled over and saw Wes apparently still asleep, a cherub in homespun, as innocent as a newborn. But looks were deceiving. Any boy who could calmly put a bullet into another person was no angel. Fargo was afraid Wes had the makings of a coldhearted killer. It depended on how his life unfolded.

Abruptly, Wes rose. "About time you woke up. I've been awake a good long while. Another couple of minutes and I was leaving without you." Standing, Wes stooped to fold his blanket. "Don't dawdle, mister. Susie needs me."

Another ordeal of heat and exhaustion had to be endured. Fargo filled the water skin before they left, yet it was so hot that taking a drink afforded little relief. Two minutes after a welcome sip, his throat would be as parched as it had been before he drank. He treated the horses to a few handfuls every few hours, and that evening filled his hat and held it to their muzzles. Not once did Wes gripe about being thirsty; the boy was as tough as a young Apache.

Little was said until they made camp. Fargo had shared more pemmican and Wes had pulled out the two derringers and was cleaning them again. To draw the boy into conversation and hopefully learn more about Susan Dixon, Fargo commented, "You treat those parlor guns as if they're made of gold."

"A good gun is the best friend we have." Fondly stroking one, Wes said, "Since I was seven I've helped put food on the supper table. Squirrels, possum, coon, deer. You name it, I've killed it. I haven't killed a man yet but it's only a matter of time."

"Not if you don't let it happen. Most people go their entire lives without killing."

31

Holding a derringer up so it glistened in the starlight, Wes wiped the barrels. "I know. But something tells me I'm not like everyone else. I've never balked at pulling the trigger and I feel no regrets after I do. What's the use of troubling yourself? Dead is dead."

Fargo couldn't imagine how a preacher's son had turned out like John Wesley. The boy was as untamable as a mustang that refused to be broken. "I hope, for your sake, you never do shoot anyone. There's no turning back. You'll get a reputation, and others will want to test whether you're worthy. So you kill them to defend yourself, feeding the tales. It's a vicious circle."

"I wouldn't mind being famous," Wes said. "Look at Cullen Baker. He's the biggest man in Texas right about now."

And one of the worst, Fargo had heard. Baker was a crack shot, a bully, and a heavy drinker. A fearsome combination. It was claimed he could unlimber a hogleg faster than anyone alive, but he usually did so while under the influence of rotgut liquor, and usually at the expense of his victim's life. The first person he was known to have killed was a farmer who objected to his bullying.

"They say he's shot seven men, maybe as many as ten," Wes boasted. "I'll bet no one tells him what to do, ever. That's how I'd like to be one day."

"You want people to be afraid of you? To have every sheriff and marshal in the state out to slap shackles on your wrists?"

"I can take care of myself. Besides, my kin will help me if I get in a fix. We always look out for one another."

Fargo gestured. "Then where are they now? Why aren't they helping you track down your cousin?"

Jumping up, Wes shook a finger at him. "Think I can't guess what you're up to? Well, it won't work. Nothing you say or do will get me to turn back. I'm the only hope Susie has." The boy was shaking from raw emotion. "As for my kinfolk, my uncle spread word he didn't want anyone going after her. And no one dares buck him. My pa sure won't, not when it's his own brother."

The boy sat back down and kept a stormy silence for the rest of the evening. Daybreak found them in the saddle. By noon they were deep in among higher hills, in a remote region Fargo had never visited, so rugged it was only fit for rattlesnakes and lizards.

A rutted dirt road they happened on guided them toward Hender's Gap. Fargo had never heard of the place but that was nothing new. Settlements sprang up all the time, some in the most out-of-the-way spots. Many withered and died as quickly as they sprouted, leaving the ghostly shells of clapboard buildings as mute testimony of their existence.

Fargo had Hender's Gap pegged as a farming or ranching settlement, probably no larger than a thimble, with a saloon and a stable. But along about sunset, from a ridge overlooking a serpentine valley, he set eyes on two dozen buildings that flanked a winding dusty street. Horses were tied to five or six hitch posts and lamps glowed in many windows.

"This is the place," Wes announced. "Susie is down there somewhere."

"You been heading here all along?" Fargo saw no farms or ranches in the valley or on any adjacent slopes. Yet how else could a town that size support itself?

Wes slapped his legs against the mare. "It shouldn't take more than an hour to find her. Thanks for all you've done for me, mister. I can handle the rest." Amid swirling puffs of dust he trotted away.

Fargo started to catch up. He didn't care to let the boy out of his sight for a minute. But he slowed to a walk rather than add to the Ovaro's fatigue, confident that in a town the size of Hender's Gap, finding Wes again wouldn't pose a problem.

The boy was halfway there before Fargo reached the valley floor and discovered a sign on a post, both so thick with dust they blended into the background and were next to invisible in the gathering gloom. It was a strange sign, painted in scrawled letters: HENDER'S GAP, FOUNDED MAY, 1859. STRANGERS ARE NOT WELCOME. LAWMEN MUST CHECK IN AT MARSHAL'S OFFICE. HENDER RULES.

What that last line meant was anybody's guess. As for strangers being frowned upon, Fargo just figured the marshal didn't want any hard cases or badmen stepping foot in town. That business about lawmen checking in was a common courtesy lawdogs extended to one another everywhere.

Tinny piano music wafted to Fargo's ears as he followed the rutted track on in. The street ran from south to north, past Hender's General Store, Hender's Hotel, Hender's Saloon, and Hender's Livery. Small shacks had sprung up like thistles between the larger structures. At the north end stood a two-story house bearing a gaudy red sign: LILY'S PLACE.

Whoever had put the buildings up must have been drunk at the time. Planks were nailed at random, with wide gaps between boards. Many of the roofs sagged, and looked as if they would collapse if a fly were to land on them. Doorjambs were uneven, the doors tilted at mad angles. Windows were worse.

Fargo reined up at the saloon. Wes's mare was in front of the general store but the boy was nowhere to be seen. Nor were many of the town's residents. An elderly man sat in a rocking chair whittling, and two women in tight dresses were talking over by Lily's. Dismounting, Fargo arched his spine to relieve a cramp, then wrapped the reins around the rail.

"Can't you read, stranger?"

The speaker wore a tarnished tin star pinned to a store-bought shirt that had more food stains on it than clean spots. A double chin covered with stubble hung low over a chest that had caved in on an ample belly. A bowler crowned his moon head. His pants were as filthy as his shirt but his boots were shined to a polish. Around his portly middle was a gun-belt bearing a matched set of Smith & Wessons.

"I saw the sign, if that's your point," Fargo said, swiping dust from his sleeve.

"And you came on in anyway? Either you're mighty bold or mighty stupid."

Fargo had taken an instant dislike to the man, and he contrived to lower his hand close to his Colt.

"I don't see a badge so you can't be a ranger. Unless you're hiding it."

"I'm no lawman," Fargo stressed, mystified as to why that should be so important. "I'm looking for a boy who rode in about five minutes ago."

"Your son?"

"A friend. I'm helping him track down a cousin of his." Fargo didn't reveal anything else. He felt that the less the lawman knew, the less nosy the man would be. But that wasn't the case.

"Oh? This cousin have a name?"

"You haven't told me who *you* are," Fargo mentioned, and gave his own name, presenting his hand to shake. After a moment's hesitation the lawman did, his grip immensely strong, a clue he was packing more muscle than flab.

"Caleb Hender. My office is yonder." Hender pointed at a shack. "I reckon you can stay, but behave. Any trouble, and my deputies and me will throw you behind bars and keep you there until you pay whatever fine the judge sets."

"Hender?" Fargo's interest perked. "Are you the founder of this town?"

"Goodness, no. That would be my pa, Ira. The whole family thought he was touched in the head, wanting to build in the middle of nowhere. But it's paid off. My cousin Sam owns the store, Charlie runs the livery, and my sister Lil has her own sporting establishment." Caleb winked.

"The deputies you mentioned, are they related, too?"

"Sure are. They're kin on my ma's side. Lester and Norman Mosely."

Now Fargo understood why Orville had laughed when he mentioned going to the law in Hender's Gap. And why Orville had said the lawman was partial to local boys. "What about the judge?"

"That would be Pa himself. He's judge, mayor, and undertaker, all rolled into one." Caleb nodded at the hotel. "He holds court there once a month, when he's of a mind. Sometimes he forgets, though. Then he has to charge prisoners extra for all their meals and board at our expense." Caleb placed his hands on his big belly. "I admit Hender's Gap doesn't look like much. But it's our town and we like to keep things nice and peaceful."

"I'm not here to cause trouble," Fargo said.

"Good. Then you can stay one whole day. By this time tomorrow, I want you on that pinto of yours and moving on."

Being bossed around always raised Fargo's dander. "If I'm not?"

Caleb's face creased in an oily smile. "If you're not, I can rustle up as many of my kinfolk as I need to hold you down while I stomp on you until you're black and blue all over. That's if I'm feelin' charitable. I might just throw you in jail for six months."

Fargo knew a stacked deck when he saw one. "I'm only interested in helping the boy. We should be done by then."

The lawman's double chin bobbed. "For your sake, I hope so. Now I'd better look up this boy you keep talkin' about and see who he's huntin'." Caleb clomped off, pudgy head held high.

The Ovaro was guzzling water from the trough. Fargo patted it, saying under his breath, "Why do I feel as if I've just fallen into a rattlesnake den?" He strolled into the saloon, pushing the batwing doors wide. Cigar smoke hung thick below the low ceiling. At the bar were seven grungy men nursing drinks. At half a dozen tables, card games were in progress. The piano was in a far corner, being pounded on by a bald fellow in a cheap suit. Four women in bright dresses were working the room, another was behind the bar with the bartender.

The moment Fargo entered, all sound died. Everyone turned toward him, and except for the women, there wasn't a friendly expression in the crowd. They were as hostile as

Comanches, some starting to move their hands toward their pistols or knives.

Acting on inspiration, Fargo announced, "All of you can relax. The marshal just gave me permission to stay." It had the desired effect. The gamblers resumed playing and the drinkers went back to sipping and jawing. A new tune jangled from the piano, masterfully mutilated by the bald man.

Fargo walked to the near end of the bar and leaned against it. The woman, not the barkeep, sashayed up to take his order. A petite brunette, she must have been beautiful once but years of jaded living had taken its toll. Still, she was the prettiest woman present, her green eyes twinkling as she rested her forearms close to his, and grinned.

"That was quick thinkin', handsome. The last stranger who waltzed in here without permission was cut up real bad before the marshal could stop it." She extended her slender hand. "Madelyn Mosely."

Yet another relative, Fargo noted. A lavender dress was molded to her ripe body, clinging to her hips and swelling amply to accommodate her full bosom. Tantalizing perfume wreathed her curly locks, tingling his nose. "Call me Skye," he said. Her palm was pleasantly warm.

"You sure are a fine-lookin' devil," Madelyn bluntly declared. As she withdrew her hand, she slid a finger across his palm in a tiny caress. "What's your poison? Coffin varnish? Or can I interest you in a private room at Lily's with all the trimmin's?" Her cherry lips parted and the pink tip of her tongue delicately rimmed them in a blatant invitation.

"Whiskey will do for now," Fargo said, "but that room sounds tempting. Maybe later on, after I've washed some of the dust down my throat."

"Come a long way, have you?" Madelyn idly asked while selecting a glass from a shelf. She inspected it, frowned, and exchanged it for another. "Ah. Here's a clean one. Most of the men around here wouldn't care if it was covered with hog snot, but I like to run a respectable establishment."

"You own the saloon?"

"Lordy, no. Ira Hender owns everything, in case you haven't heard. But he lets me run it, just like he lets his son Charley run the livery and his daughter Lily run the bawdy house." Madelyn lowered her voice. "But where they get a percentage of all the money they make, I get fifty measly dollars a month and free board."

The bitterness in her tone was thick enough to cut with a butter knife. "Why is it they get more than you?" Fargo asked.

"I'm just a Mosely," Madelyn responded. "My aunt is Ira's wife. Which doesn't count for much in his book. Moselys are fit to be deputies but not marshals. Moselys are fit to sweep out the stable but never in a million years to take charge of it. See a pattern there, handsome?"

"If you're that unhappy, why not leave?"

Fleeting sadness sagged Madelyn's shoulders. "If only it were that simple. But Ira doesn't take kindly to kin who try and walk out on him. The last one who did, his own nephew, was tied to a post and whipped until his back was cut to ribbons."

Fargo accepted the shot of red-eye and swallowed half in one gulp, relishing the burning sensation that oozed into the pit of his stomach. Ira Hender wasn't so much a family patriarch as a petty tyrant, ruthlessly lording it over his own little domain. His own family was the royalty and everyone else lowly peons, even the Moselys, their cousins. "It's not right," he declared.

Madelyn looked at him. "No, it's not," she answered softly so no one else could overhear. "But if you ever tell anyone else I said that, I'll deny it. Ira isn't above beatin' a woman when he thinks she needs to learn a lesson."

Leaning forward so his mouth brushed her earlobe, Fargo whispered, "You're welcome to come with me when I go. I can take you as far as Santa Fe."

"Oh, if only I dared!" Madelyn clasped his left hand in hers. "But if we were caught, you'd be guest of honor at a hemp social. I thank you for your kind offer, though." Her fingers artfully stroked his. "Are you sure I can't tempt you into visitin' Lily's? Just you and me, alone?" She actually blushed. "I don't usually throw myself at customers this way, but I've taken a real shine to you."

Under other circumstances Fargo would like nothing better. But he had the boy to think of, and he had delayed too long as it was. Cupping her chin, he said, "I have some business to attend to. Then I'll be back. And if your offer still holds, I'll take you up on it."

"Oh, I'm not liable to change my—" Madelyn stopped. Her gaze had drifted beyond him to the entrance, and she stiffened.

Fargo turned.

Framed in the doorway was Caleb Hender. He was scowling, his pudgy hands resting on the Smith & Wessons. Tramping toward the bar, he growled, "Just what in hell are you tryin' to pull, mister?"

## 4

Skye Fargo could have heard spit hit the floorboards. Every-one had stopped what they were doing and shifted to see why the lawman was so upset. Fargo wanted to know the same, so he asked.

"I think maybe you lied to me. I think maybe you're here for some other reason than helpin' a kid." Caleb planted himself like a mad bull about to charge. "I don't like being made a fool of."

"His horse is in front of the general store so he has to be here somewhere," Fargo replied. "Ask him yourself and he'll confirm what I told you."

"That's just it. I asked at the store and I asked old Wattie, who never leaves his rocking chair across the street. No one saw a kid ride in. The only person who's showed up in the past couple of hours is you."

Fargo polished off the whiskey and smacked the glass down. "I'll find him myself." He headed for the batwings but Caleb's thick fingers wrapped around his wrist. They locked eyes.

"Not so fast. You'll go when I say you can." The lawdog was puffed up like a porcupine bristling for a fight.

Fargo's gaze drilled into Caleb like twin daggers. No one else was interfering. Slowly, Caleb's grip slackened. Finally, he removed his hand and nervously coughed.

"We'll go look for the boy together. And if it turns out you weren't telling the truth, you'd better have a damn good excuse."

Twilight cloaked the valley and the temperature had dropped a few degrees but not enough to be comfortable. Old Wattie, Fargo saw, was no longer in the rocking chair. The two women outside Lily's had also disappeared. Coincidence? he wondered. Or convenience? He made a beeline for the store and was almost there before it hit him that Wes's mare wasn't tied to the hitch rail. Nor was it at any of the others.

Hender's General Store could just as well have been named Hender's Pigsty. The place was a mess, articles and clothes piled in heaps or jammed onto shelves in no particular order. None of it was new merchandise. Dresses, tools, odds and ends, tack, wagon parts, all were worn or rusty or splotched with dirt. A thin man about thirty years of age, whose left eyelid constantly twitched, appeared from among the junk, wiping his scrawny hands on a frayed apron. "How-do, mister. What can I get you?"

"You're Sam," Fargo guessed.

"How did you know?" Sam responded amiably enough.

Just then Caleb Hender waddled across the threshold. "I told him, cousin. He's the one I was just tellin' you about, the one who claims he's here with some boy."

"Oh. Him." Sam's thin smile evaporated like dew. "Well, like I said before, the only boys who paid me a visit today were Josephine's two scamps and Esmeralda's little Joey."

"His name is Wes," Fargo said. "He's ten or eleven going on twenty. His mare was hitched right outside your store a while ago."

Sam moved to the counter and fiddled with a jar of tacks. "I can't be bothered to check on every jasper who ties up out front. I'm a busy man. Busy, busy, busy." He motioned at a door on the right wall. "Most of the day I've been in there takin' inventory. It's possible your little friend came in and I never saw him."

"Could be," Fargo conceded, although Sam didn't strike

him as the kind to miss much. Yet there was no denying the boy was gone. The question was, where? Not to the saloon. Certainly not to the bawdy house, as Madelyn had branded it. That left the livery and the hotel as the likeliest prospects.

"Well?" Caleb said smugly. "Ready to admit you lied?"

"Ready to eat your teeth?" Fargo countered, and shouldered past him. The hotel was closest. He angled across the dusty street and into a small, spartan lobby dominated by a chandelier that seemed as out of place as a silk purse in a sow's ear. A mousy clerk whose spectacles magnified the size of his eyes looked up from a ledger he was scribbling in.

"Let me guess," Fargo said before the clerk opened his mouth. "Another Hender?"

"Jonathan Hender, sir, at your service." Like Sam, Jonathan's pleasant manner changed drastically when Caleb barreled in and glared at Fargo. "See here. What's going on?"

Once again Fargo explained about Wes. The proprietor hadn't seen him either.

"And I've been at the front desk since noon, going over my books," Jonathan said. "No one could come or go without my noticing." He flourished a quill pen. "How about you? Care to rent a room for the night? I have plenty of vacancies."

Caleb intervened. "This one won't be stayin' that long, brother."

"You gave me until tomorrow at sunset," Fargo reminded him.

"That's when I took you for a harmless stray. Now I'm not so sure." The lawman tapped his badge. "This tin star gives me the right to change my mind any damn time I please. So you have one hour. Unless you find the boy and bring him by my office, I'm runnin' you out of town." Hitching at his gunbelt, he departed in a huff.

Jonathan cleared his throat. "You'll have to forgive him, mister. He's a mite testy at times, but only because he takes his job seriously." He closed the ledger with a crisp snap. "I'm sorry I can't rent you a room. But we have to do as Caleb says."

His frustration climbing, Fargo went back outside. Soon it would be too dark to see much of anything. He hurried to the livery and heard someone whistling. A husky specimen in overalls was forking hay to horses in the stalls. Arms corded with sinew flicked the pitchfork as effortlessly as if it were Jonathan's quill pen. Fargo saw no trace of the mare.

The man with the pitchfork paused in midswing. "Didn't see you there, stranger. I'm Charley Hender. What can I do for you? Have a horse you need tended?"

Fargo related the bare essentials, concluding with, "I thought for sure the boy brought his mare here. Now I don't know where to look."

"Come to think of it, I do seem to recollect seein' a kid ride in just before sunset. But I didn't pay much attention to where he went or what he did."

Thanking him, Fargo walked out and to the northeast corner, which was plunged in shadow. Hunkering, he folded his arms and took stock. One fact was clear. Wes hadn't vanished into thin air. Nor would the boy leave without Susie Dixon. This insight caused Fargo to slap his forehead. *Why hadn't he realized it sooner?* The key to finding Wes was Wes's cousin. If he could locate her, he could locate the boy.

On the verge of rising, Fargo stayed still when he heard hooves thudding. A quartet of lanky riders materialized out of the gathering murk. They passed within twenty feet, unaware of him, and drew rein directly in front of the livery. A grizzled character in a broad-brimmed hat and a baggy shirt flapped a hand.

"Charley! Charley Hender! Get your lard ass out here and take care of our critters!"

It surprised Fargo that the big man bustled to do as he was bid, without protest. The foursome dismounted, their crotchety leader shoving his reins at Charley in open contempt. "Still shoveling horse crap for a living, are you?" He sniffed loudly. "How you can stand the smell is beyond me."

The other three laughed. Cold, cruel laughs.

"I do what my pa tells me," Charley said. "You know that, One-Eared John."

Fargo started. One-Eared John was at the top of the Rangers' Most Wanted list. The list of vile crimes he had committed was as long as a lariat. Rape, murder, torture. Pick an unspeakable act, and One-Eared John had done it. His nickname, so the story went, came from the fact he had lost an ear to Comanches.

"The great toad belches and you lick off the slobber, is that it?" the outlaw responded, much to the amusement of his partners.

Charley didn't share their view. "Don't talk about Pa like that. He's always done right by you, hasn't he?"

"I've got no complaints. But then, I'd better not have. I'm paying him close to a thousand a year just so the boys and me can come and go as we please, no questions asked. Same as all the others."

"Well, some don't pay that much," Charley commented.

One-Eared John was turning to go but he stopped short, his profile cast in grim relief by the lantern light spilling from the livery. "How's that again? I thought we all paid the same amount."

"Oh, no sir." Charley said. "How much it is depends on how badly you're wanted. Or something like that."

"Is that so?"

"Yes. Take Pecos Jim. All he's ever done was rob a few people. Would it be fair for him to pay as much as you when the bounty on his head isn't a tenth of what it is on yours?" Charley smiled. "Pa always likes to do right by folks."

"I reckon I need to talk with that old man of yours," One-Eared John declared. "Is he at the usual place?"

Charley grew anxious. "What for? Why are you upset? I thought you knew how the setup worked."

"Not all the particulars, from the sound of it." To his companions, One-Eared John said, "Let's go pay the toad a little visit, boys. Maybe set him straight about a few things." They moved off.

"Wait!" Charley cried. "Let me put these horses inside and I'll go with you!"

The killer and his pack of curly wolves didn't look back. "We don't need no nursemaid. You go about your business and we'll go about ours."

In the shadows, Fargo rose. He watched Charley fidget and then hustle into the livery. Quickly, Fargo trailed the quartet, hugging the buildings on the right side of the street so he wouldn't be detected. The four hard cases made for the hotel. But instead of going in, they filed into an alley between the hotel and some shacks that flanked it and walked on around to the rear.

Fargo waited a full minute before following them. The hotel was the longest structure in town, by far. At the back was another hitch rail with four mounts tied up. That in itself was unusual. Even more so was a wooden ramp that ran from the hitch rail to an oversized door. A large window had been fitted with glass, a rare treat in that part of the country. Purple drapes had been drawn but not quite all the way, and light seeped from the edges.

Checking both ways, Fargo stepped from concealment and squatted to peek inside. He saw shadows play across a wall but couldn't spot anyone. Muffled voices buzzed.

On his hands and knees Fargo moved to the other side of the window. Here the voices were louder, the crack between the drape and the sill wider. He peered in, and was dumbfounded. In his wide-flung travels he had seen many strange sights, but few to rival that which he now beheld.

A spacious chamber, as large as nine or ten normal hotel rooms combined, was lavishly adorned with every luxury known to man. There was mahogany furniture, polished to a sheen. Sofas fitted with plump cushions. A table long enough to seat twenty. Plush carpet inches thick. But what furniture! What sofas! Each was three times as large as it should be, while the chair at the head of the table was wide enough for the Ovaro to sit in. It was a chamber fit for a giant—or an ogre.

On the left was an enormous divan, and sprawled on it was the person for whom the furniture had been custom-made. To call him huge did not do him justice. He was gigantic, a great, obscene slug of a man whose flesh bulged against his clothes in unseemly folds of overlapping excess. His arms and legs were short in comparison to his bulk, and as deformed as the rest of him. A pumpkin face harbored dark saucer eyes above a cavernous mouth lined by uneven teeth.

It could only be Ira Hender. Without a doubt, he was the single most repulsive human being Fargo had ever laid eyes on. Fargo had heard tell that people his size often died young, their hearts unable to take the strain of such massive bodies. But the head of the Hender clan had to be in his fifties.

At Ira's elbow stood Caleb. Five younger men armed with rifles were positioned close to the divan to protect their lord and master. Confronting them was One-Eared John and his friends, while off to one side stood Madelyn Mosely, her expression making it evident she would rather be anywhere else than where she was.

One-Eared John was speaking. "—taking advantage of me, damn your bones, and I don't like it. Not one bit. I want my amount cut in half, which is still more than you and your brood deserve."

Ira's voice rumbled with power. "Is that so? Where else in all of Texas can you go and be safe? Completely, utterly safe? Name just one place, one town, one settlement, and I'll gladly cut the amount here and now."

"You know very well I can't. Wanted posters of me are plastered on half the buildings and trees in the state."

"So Hender's Gap is your only safe haven?" Ira clucked like a flustered hen. "Yet you stand there and haggle over how much priceless sanctuary costs you. I offer you a rare gift and you accuse me of greed."

The killer took a step but changed his mind when Caleb and the guards all visibly tensed. "I'm not accusing you of anything, Ira. All I'm saying is that I don't think it's fair I pay so much more than everybody else."

The elder Hender sat back, a sausage arm rising to scratch his cauliflower ear. "Let's go over our arrangement again. You don't appear to understand exactly how it works." One-Eared John went to interrupt but Ira silenced him with a gesture. "This town is mine, lock, stock, and barrel. My kin run every business. Some live in outlyin' ranches and cabins, sent there by me to keep their eyes skinned for strangers." Ira slowly sat up. "No one can come or go without my knowledge. Lawmen who wander in are met by my son, Caleb. And if they're after someone who happens to have paid for sanctuary, he makes sure the lawmen go on their merry way empty-handed."

One-Eared John couldn't contain himself. "I know all that, damn you!"

"But do you appreciate its value?" Ira said. "While you're here, no one will arrest you. No one will try to gun you down. My family keeps you as safe as you were in your mother's womb. And for this invaluable service I ask a paltry thousand dollars a year."

"Paltry?" One-Eared John exploded. "Money doesn't grow on cactus, you toad! I have to work hard to steal that much. So cut my amount, or else."

"Toad?" Ira repeated, his lower lip thrusting out. For a bit he was quiet, then he sighed. "I see. I've misjudged you, John. I thought you were smart enough to know a good deal when you found one."

"Now hold on—"

For someone so immense, Ira could move swiftly when he wanted. And now he reared up off the divan, his stubby legs somehow supporting his bulk. "No, *you* hold on. I've offered you the hospitality of my town, my family, my home. And what do you do? You insult me. You threaten me. You make demands of me." Ira sighed again. "Some folks just don't know when they're well off."

Fargo saw Madelyn sidling toward a sofa.

Ira did an odd thing. He held up four fingers that were all the same length, and wriggled them. "A man with a six-thousand-dollar bounty on his head shouldn't make undue demands, John. You're now worth more to me dead than you are alive. Boys, if you'd please do the honors."

Much too late, the four outlaws realized their peril. One-Eared John stabbed at his pistol but the guards already had their rifles tucked to their shoulders. Madelyn ducked behind the sofa as a volley rang out. The four outlaws never got off a shot, never even touched their hardware. Each was cored through the head and fell where he stood, the blasts pealing like thunder.

Fargo felt no sympathy for John or the rest. They were brutal killers, plain and simple, and they had reaped a justly deserved fate, the same fate they'd inflicted on so many innocents over the years.

Ira Hender made a teepee of his hands. "I do so detest fools. Caleb, you'll see to the reward money?"

"Of course, Pa."

"Hiram, go fetch a bunch of your cousins and have them tote the bodies out. All but John are to be fed to the coyotes. Get Lester to chop off John's right hand so if anyone doubts he's dead, we'll have proof. Then hang the body from that tree north of town as a warning to anyone else who might be tempted to prod me."

One of the young guards nodded and hastened through a door on the far side of the chamber.

"Now then," Ira said, "on to that other problem, the one we were talkin' about when these Texans rudely barged in. Madelyn? Where are you, dear?"

The brunette showed herself. "Playing it safe," she answered. "Next time, give a gal a little more warning, will you?"

"You saw the signal so don't be sassin' me. Remember your cousin Clara."

Madelyn paled. "I still think cuttin' out her tongue was uncalled for. She never did get over it. That's why she jumped off that cliff."

Ira crooked a finger and Madelyn timidly advanced until she was just out of his reach. He chuckled, causing the heavy folds of his flesh to ripple like the coils of a snake. "Look at her, Caleb. I do believe the poor dear is scared to death of me. Me! Her own kin. Her own uncle by marriage. Now why would that be, do you suppose?"

Caleb sneered. "Is it fear, Pa? Or just that she's always felt she was too good for us? Her with her books and her poetry and all."

"Now, now," Ira said. "Learnin' to read is worth the bother. Look at Jonathan, Sam, and you. I had to take switches to your backsides when you were little to get you to do it. But those welts have paid off." Ira paused. "You could have a point, though. If there's one thing I've learned in life, boy, it's that too much education is bad as sin for females. They get all kinds of contrary notions into their heads."

Fargo didn't need to hear any more. He risked being found if he lingered. But as he straightened, Madelyn said something that glued him there.

"Did you send for me to talk about my shortcoming, Ira, or the stranger who came into the saloon today?"

"Skye Fargo, yes," Ira said severely. "I understand you had an intimate chat with him. The two of you were holdin' hands and whisperin' like lovers, is how it was described."

Madelyn forced a laugh that sounded false even to Fargo. "Oh, please. It's my job to make customers feel welcome. To ply them with drinks so they spend more money. I didn't treat him any differently than I do every other man."

"I'll take your word for it, for now. But tell me, what was it the two of you talked about?"

"Oh, the usual. The weather. Whether he'd like to take a

room at Lily's. He wasn't in the saloon more than a couple of minutes when Caleb marched in as mad as a wet hen, and Fargo left."

"He never mentioned Sline or Susan Dixon?"

"No."

Caleb had been listening impatiently. "What about the boy? Did he say anything about someone named Wes?"

The backhand blow that caught the lawman across the cheek sent him staggering into the divan. Caleb had to cling to it in order to remain on his feet. Beet red, he sputtered like a geyser, then whined, "What in tarnation did you do that for, Pa? All I did was ask her about the kid."

Ira sank onto the divan and stretched his stubby arms across the back of it, a king at his leisure. "I do the askin', not you, son. The less anyone else knows about this, the better. But now you've gone and whetted her curiosity. Think, boy. Think. The key to success in life is usin' your head."

"Who is this Wes?" Madelyn inquired.

Ira looked at Caleb. "See what I mean?" To her, he said, "He's none of your concern, my dear. A minor nuisance, is all. And Sam has seen to it that he will be properly attended to." Ira stroked his chin. "No, our main problem is Fargo."

"He's just one man," Caleb said. "What can he do?"

"You're not thinkin' again, boy. That name of his. Skye Fargo. It's not a handle you hear every day. Surely it rings a bell? He's the one folks talk about a lot, the scout, the plainsman. He's very dangerous."

"Between the Henders and the Moselys we can muster upwards of two dozen guns. He'll be worm food quicker than you can blink, Pa."

Ira looked at Madelyn. "See what happens? You give your pride and joy a position of authority and he becomes a know-it-all." Ira's pumpkin face scrunched up in rebuke. "Son, when will you learn? It isn't numbers that count, it's cleverness. If the Texas Rangers or the U.S. Marshals got wind of what we're up to, they'd send in a hundred men and wipe us out."

Caleb still didn't understand. "What's that got to do with Fargo?"

"Use your pitiful excuse for a brain. He claims he's here to help that whelp. But what if there's more to it? What if he's nosin' around to learn what we're up to? I know for a fact he's worked for the army before. What if they sent him to spy on us?"

"We kill him and bury him in the hills where they'll never find the body," Caleb responded. "End of problem."

Ira glanced down at himself and remarked, "Sometimes it's mighty hard for me to believe you are the fruit of my loins. I've always had the naggin' notion that you resemble my brother Thaddeus more than you do me. When I see your ma later, I'm going to wallop her just for the hell of it."

"I wish you'd quit insultin' me, Pa."

"Then *think*!" Ira practically roared. "If the government did send him in, they'd be suspicious if he never reported back. They'd send in a patrol to snoop around. And we don't want that, do we?"

"No, I reckon not."

Outside, Fargo backed away from the window. Paying the nearest ranger headquarters or federal marshal's office a visit wasn't a bad idea. Let them deal with the nest of vermin. But he had to find Wes before he left, and he still had no clue where to start. Or did he? Almost to the opening between buildings, he began to pivot.

Without warning, an arm as thick as a tree trunk wrapped around Fargo's neck and clamped him like a vise. Almost at the same instant another arm seized him around the chest, pinning his own arms to his sides, and he was lifted bodily off the ground.

"I came after One-Eared John and saw you spyin' on my pa, mister," Charley Hender said gruffly. "I've been waitin' for the chance to jump you. Now, what say we go have a little talk with him?" The muscular liveryman moved toward the ramp, carrying Fargo as easily as most men would a baby.

Fargo whipped his head forward, then drove it back against Charley's face. Cartilage crunched, and Charley grunted but didn't let go. Thrashing, Fargo slammed his boots against Charley's shins. Once, twice, three times, and at the last blow, the liveryman uttered a ferocious growl and hurled him to the earth.

Fargo had to finish the fight quickly. The commotion was bound to attract Ira's guards. He sprang erect and swung a fist at Charley's square jaw but the liveryman flicked out his hand, catching Fargo's fist in midair as a youngster would catch a ball. Fingers chiseled from stone squeezed Fargo's knuckles near to bursting.

Fargo kicked at Charley's groin. He connected, yet it was like kicking a wall, and the next thing he knew, Charley had pulled him close and seized his throat in the other hand. His jugular felt fit to rupture.

"You shouldn't have hurt me, mister. Now I'm going to hurt you. Hurt you so you won't forget."

The darkness blurred, the buildings spun. Fargo couldn't breathe, couldn't break free. He sagged, going limp. The worst that could happen, had happened, and unless he was a magician, Caleb might get to bury him off in the hills, after all. As if to hammer the point home, he heard the lawman shout.

"What the hell is going on out there?"

# 5

Desperation sparks inspiration.

Skye Fargo was on the verge of passing out when for a moment Charley Hender's face swam into focus above him. Marshaling his strength, Fargo lunged upward, gouging Charley in the eyes and raking them with his fingernails. A howl loud enough to be heard in San Antonio ripped from the liveryman, and he let go. As Fargo sucked air into his lungs, Charley backpedaled, fingers splayed over his bleeding eyes.

"I'm blind! You've blinded me!"

Fargo doubted it. He whirled just as the door opened, and saw one of the guards. The man levered a rifle up but Fargo was swifter. The Colt leaped from its holster, stabbing flame and lead. Two slugs smashed into the guard's chest and he was hurled inward, against others rushing to get out.

Fargo ran north, vaulting over the ramp. He had to get to the Ovaro and get out of town before they thought to cut him off. At the corner he plunged into a narrow alley between the hotel and another building but he had only gone a few steps when a gangly silhouette appeared at the other end.

"Hey there! What's all that hollerin' and shoutin' about?"

Spinning on a boot heel, Fargo reversed direction. Two of Ira's watchdogs had emerged but they were facing Charley, who continued to wail at the top of his lungs. Fargo sprinted to the north again, toward the next inky alley. He was almost there when a rifle banged and a leaden hornet buzzed by his ear. Rotating, he thumbed off a shot, saw a rifleman fall, and was into the alley in a bound.

"After him! Get that bastard or there will be hell to pay!"

Caleb's voice. Soon every Hender and Mosely in town would converge on the scene. Fargo dashed toward the street but slowed before exposing himself. It was well he did. Two riflemen raced into the street further down, and eight or nine other people were hurrying toward the hotel. More materialized in doorways and peered from windows.

"What's going on?" someone shouted.

"Why all the shootin'?" quizzed another.

One of Ira's bodyguards answered. "Spread out! We're lookin' for that big feller in buckskins, the one who rode in on a pinto!"

Fargo glanced toward the hitch rail where he had left the Ovaro and received a shock. It was gone! Someone had taken it! Whether it was one of the Henders or one of the outlaws who paid them for sanctuary was irrelevant. Now he had no way out of town unless he stole someone else's mount. Which he decided he would do, then come back later after things had quieted down.

Three horses were tied to another rail to the north. Pulling his hat low and tucking his chin to his chest, Fargo glided along the wall. More and more people were showing up every second. In no time the street would be a teeming throng.

A door ahead abruptly opened and out walked two hard cases. They stepped to the hitch rail to better observe the goings-on, one saying to the other, "What do you suppose all the fuss is about?"

"Don't rightly know. But I don't like it. Ira promised us peace and quiet. This ruckus can't be a good sign."

Fargo walked on by the pair. Trying to take one of their horses with them standing there would bring the whole bunch down on his head. Neither paid him any mind, and at the next corner he paused to debate what to do next.

"Gather around! Gather around, everyone! We're going to search this town from end to end!"

That was Caleb again, in front of the hotel now, at the center of the swelling crowd.

Fargo kept walking until he came to the last shack. Beyond was open grassland. To the right, across the street, its gaudy sign bathed in light that filtered from the house, was Lily's Place. Of all the dwellings in Hender's Gap, only her bawdy house had a picket fence around it. It was also the only property with a flower garden, although most of the plants were shriveled. Of special interest to Fargo were the shrubs planted along the side. They had grown to shoulder height, high enough to hide behind.

Angling to the gate, Fargo hurried toward the porch. There were women at four of the windows but they were staring toward the hotel. He veered off and was in among the shrubs before any of them noticed. Squatting with his back to the wall, he watched as Caleb divided the searchers into two groups—sending one to the livery, and leading the other toward the north end, toward Lily's.

Fargo retreated to the rear of the house. An open window was within reach and he rose on his toes to see in. The room was empty. He knew better than to climb inside and hide. Caleb would poke into every closet, look under every bed.

The high grass beckoned. Thankfully, the moon wasn't out. Fargo placed a hand on top of the picket fence and jumped over, then jogged out a good twenty yards. Turning, he flattened his body to the ground, drew the Colt, and reloaded.

A hubbub in front of Lily's signaled that Caleb and company had arrived, and soon women and their customers were screeching and bellowing in outrage at the intrusion. Through some of the windows Fargo could see the searchers going from room to room.

Then torches flared, held aloft by men who prowled the shrubs and trampled the flower garden. They crisscrossed the entire yard and wound up at the back fence. Among them was the walking outhouse who wore a tin badge.

"He ain't here, Caleb. Let's move on," a tall searcher suggested.

"Not so fast, Zeb. Ira wants this varmint, wants him bad. Six of you take torches and make a sweep of the grass."

"How far out?" Zeb asked.

"A hundred yards or so, all the way around the town."

Grumbling ensued, Zeb protesting loudest of all. "Hell, that'll take a couple of hours! Why don't we wait until after the sun comes up and do it on horseback? We can cover the whole valley in that amount of time."

"I want it done now," Caleb commanded. "Or else you can go explain to Ira why you'd rather not, and we'll let him decide."

"No, no," Zeb said. "We shouldn't bother your pa. If it has to be done, it has to be done." Zeb pointed at five of the men. "You're elected to help me, boys. Fan out. Thirty steps apart." He glanced at the lawman. "You haven't said. Does Ira want this polecat alive or bucked out in gore?"

"We'd like him to answer a few questions. Shoot him full of holes if you have to, but try to keep him breathin'. If you can't, don't fret. Pa won't hold it against anyone." Caleb gestured, and everyone else followed him toward the street.

Zeb frowned. "Well, you heard the man. Let's get this over with." Those he'd chosen spread out in a long line. When Zeb waved his torch, they waded into the grass with revolvers leveled.

Fargo hadn't budged. He couldn't possibly get more than a hundred yards out without being spotted. He marked where the men were in relation to where he was, and deduced that only one would pass uncomfortably close, on the right. Exercising supreme care, he crawled to the left. He figured on stopping when he was halfway to the next gunman but they advanced a lot faster than he'd anticipated. He had only gone five yards when flickering torchlight played over him.

Pressed flat, Fargo froze. The man on the right was swinging his torch back and forth, doing a thorough job. Fargo trained the Colt on him but didn't fire. Not yet. Not unless it was absolutely necessary.

"Give a shout if you see anything suspicious!" Zeb instructed him. "Remember, he's already killed two of our kin tonight. We don't want to make it three."

"Who is this hombre we're after?" asked the one closest to Fargo. "What do you know about him, cousin?"

"Not much, Rufus. Word is that he might be workin' for the government. Maybe the army. Orville and Theo should have known better than to kill that trooper two months ago."

"They were only doing what Ira sent them to do. Keep an eye on the trail from the east, and not let anyone by who might give us grief."

"But Caleb told me that soldier-boy was only passin' through, headin' to a new post. We're damned lucky a patrol wasn't sent to look for him."

"Why didn't one come, you reckon?"

Zeb shrugged, his torch dipping up and down. "How should I know? Maybe the soldier-boy was cuttin' across country and never told anyone the route he'd take."

By now the line was almost abreast of Fargo. Rufus wasn't more than ten feet away, intent as a bloodhound. But Fargo's buckskins blended into the brown grass so well that Rufus would have to be right on top of him to see him. Fargo avoided staring at the man's torch so its glow wouldn't reflect in his eyes.

"I don't see how this feller got into town without being seen," remarked a short cutthroat. "If he came from the east, Theo should have spotted him. If he came from the west, Deke would have."

"Not everybody uses regular trails or roads," Zeb said. "Some favor the high lines."

Rufus unexpectedly stopped. "Here! What's this!"

Fargo was poised to leap up shooting, but Rufus darted in the opposite direction and kicked at a dark clump.

"What is it?" Zeb shouted.

"Just some damned weeds. I thought it was his head."

The short man laughed. "Maybe you need spectacles, Rufe, like Jonathan. We'll give you a new nickname. Four-Eyes, instead of Limp-Pecker."

"And maybe you'd like me to take an ax and turn you into a gelding," Rufus replied. "Horace, you wish you'd bedded half as many females as I have."

"Sheep don't count."

Zeb swore at both of them. "This is a manhunt, not a Sunday social, you simpletons! Quit jawin' and pay attention or you're liable to be pushin' up some of this grass come mornin'."

They drifted on by. Fargo remained where he was until they were fifty yards out, when, bent at the waist, he jogged to the picket fence, swung over it, and was soon amid the shrubs again. He was content to hide there until the hunt ended, but soft weeping from the open window pulled him to the sill.

Madelyn Mosely was on the bed, her face buried in her arms, crying her heart out. Every so often she would rail, "Damn him! Damn him!" then shed a new torrent of tears.

Fargo gripped the edge to pull himself up but suddenly the door swung open and another woman came in. She was six feet tall or better, and superbly sculpted in proportion to her height. A black dress, slit clear to her thighs, complimented long raven tresses. Her lips were painted red, her cheeks a bright pink. Sashaying to the bed, she poked Madelyn in the shoulder. "What's this I hear? Why are you blubberin' like a baby when you should be over at the saloon workin'?"

Madelyn raised her head and sniffled. Tears moistened her cheeks, her chin, her neck. Including a large welt below her left eye. "See what he did? Do you see, Lily?"

Fargo gave the newcomer a second scrutiny. So this was Lily Hender, Ira's daughter. Fortunately for her, she shared none of her father's features. She was quite the beauty, even if she did go heavy on the cosmetics.

"So Pa slapped you? So what? Lord, if I had a dollar for all the times he hit me when I was growin' up, I'd be rich enough to own a mansion in New Orleans."

Teeth clenched, Madelyn hurled herself up off the bed. "I don't care who he is! No man lays a hand on me!"

"Calm down, will you? You'll be fine in a few days."

"That's not the point!" Madelyn was shaking from the intensity of her emotion. "I won't stand for being beaten. Maybe you're used to it but I'm not. So help me, if he ever slaps me around again, I'll—"

"Hush, now!" Lily put a hand over her cousin's mouth and pushed Madelyn back onto the bed. "Don't say anything you'll regret. Remember, Pa has ears everywhere. And he doesn't take kindly to being criticized behind his back."

Tears gushed anew as Madelyn clasped her arms to her chest. "I don't know how you've put up with it all these years. I truly don't. You're a lot stronger than I am."

"Nonsense. I've just had more practice being abused." Lily patted the smaller woman's shoulder. "What you need is a little time to yourself. Rest here a couple of hours. I'll fill in at the saloon. Come spell me when you're ready."

Madelyn nodded numbly. "I'm grateful. I truly am. A little rest would do me a world of good."

"I'll leave word you're not to be disturbed."

Lily swirled out, and once she was gone, Madelyn collapsed on her side and gave free reign to her sorrow. She was crying so loudly, she never heard Fargo's leg bump the sill or his boots scrape the floor. Her hands were over her face so she didn't notice when he moved to the door and threw the wooden bolt, then took a seat in the room's only chair.

Shouts outside indicated the searchers were moving slowly southward from building to building. Since they had already checked Lily's Place, Fargo was safer there than anywhere else. Finding Wes, he regretted, must wait until later. He wouldn't do the boy any good dead. As for the Ovaro, in the West, stealing a man's horse earned the culprit a bullet or a cottonwood jig. And Fargo had plenty of ammunition.

Madelyn's sobs tapered to low whimpers. Dabbing her eyes and nose with a sleeve, she sat up and said to herself, "When will I learn? I should have taken that handsome devil up on his offer."

"It still holds," Fargo said.

The brunette yipped like a scared fox. Clutching her bosom, she blurted, "You! Where did you come from? How did you get in here?"

"Yell a little louder, why don't you?" Fargo said, grinning. "They probably didn't hear you down at the hotel."

"My God!" Madelyn glanced at the door, saw that it was latched, then scampered to the window, shut it, and pulled the curtains. Happiness and anxiety fought for control over her countenance as she rushed to the chair. "I can't believe it! The whole town is after you, and there you sit, as calm as can be! Are you loco?"

"No more loco than you are, working for a son of a bitch like Ira Hender." Fargo pointed at the welt. "What did you do to deserve that?"

Madelyn touched it. "It was after you shot those two guards and ran off. Someone hollered that you were getting away. I made the mistake of smiling."

Fargo rose, standing so close to her their bodies were only inches apart. He could feel the warmth her luscious form radiated. Gently, he stroked the welt. "Ira has a lot to answer for."

"I don't want to talk about him," Madelyn said. "What about you? What will you do next?"

"We both have some time to kill." Fargo's finger drifted to her rosy lips and traced their outline. "I'll leave it to you to decide, but I know what I'd like." He didn't really expect her to, not in her state, but she mewed like a kitten and threw her arms around his neck, her breasts mashing against his chest as her mouth hungrily sought his. She tasted of whiskey and salt and mint. Her nails dug deep, especially when his tongue entwined with hers in a silken dance.

Fargo cupped her firm bottom and kneaded her nether cheeks. Cooing like a dove, Madelyn ground her hips against him, against his hardening manhood. As his forefinger slid between her legs, her breath became molten fire. His other hand undid the top of her dress, granting access to the exquisite charms underneath.

"Ohhhhhh, I want you," Madelyn husked when they parted for breath. She rubbed her cheek against his face, his neck.

Fargo shared the sentiment. His fingers delved in under her lacy undergarments to cover her left breast. Her nipple was a spike against his palm. He tweaked it, and she gasped and arched her spine, then locked her burning mouth on his and sucked on him as if he were sweet candy. Devoting himself to her breasts, he made them swell like ripe melons.

The sensual sensation of her grinding body had him as rigid as a redwood. Fargo was delighted when her hand dropped down and she brazenly took hold of his member. Waves of pleasure rippled outward. Inadvertently, he groaned, and she took that as her cue to stroke up and down in a slow, languid motion. It was all he could do to keep from erupting then and there.

Tucking at the knees, Fargo scooped her into his arms and carried her to the bed. She writhed seductively as he set her down, her dress sliding up over her knees to reveal a tantalizing glimpse of ivory thighs.

"Help me forget, handsome. For a little while, at least. Help me forget my whole sorry existence." Madelyn reached up and delicately ran a fingertip over his right ear. "And when you leave, take me with you. I can't take any more of this. I'm not like the rest of my kin. I've always been different. I like to imagine a better life. Or maybe I just have too much pride. I won't grovel at that monster's feet. I wo—"

"Shhhh," Fargo said. She was talking faster and faster and was about to burst into tears again. "You jabber worse than a chipmunk."

Laughing, Madelyn hooked her hands behind her neck. "Lordy, you are adorable. Do you know that?"

"Babies are adorable. Men are just horny." Smiling, Fargo lowered himself to the bed. She snuggled against him, her mouth greedily meeting his, their kiss lingering for what seemed like forever while his hands aroused her to a fever pitch. He caressed her soft neck, the slope of her shoulders. He parted her dress and her lacy undergarments to reveal magnificent breasts. And when the kiss finally ended, he lowered his mouth to her right nipple.

"Umm, yesssssss," Madelyn breathed. Removing his hat, she dropped it on the floor and grasped him by the hair. "You're making me so hot."

Fargo was only getting started. He gave her other breast the same attention, his hands roaming down her legs to her knees and then up along her inner thighs. They were cool to the touch, pliant and satiny. As he stroked up and down, they grew warmer and warmer, like kindling ignited by friction. Madelyn began to move her hips in uninhibited abandon.

"Now!" she said. "I want you buried in me now."

Fargo wasn't ready yet. Instead, he brushed a finger between her thighs. At the contact of his hand, she cried out and rose up off the bed as if she were striving to fly through the ceiling. When she sank back down, Fargo delved his finger deeper, up into her core.

Madelyn stiffened, gasped, and squirmed. Her inner walls rippled and contracted as his finger swirled around and around. "Ahhhh! So soon! So soon!" The lower half of her body flung against him, her head thrown back with her mouth wide.

Fargo inhaled her musky, tantalizing fragrance. It goaded him into sinking to his knees between her legs, into gluing his mouth where his finger had explored, into sucking on her there as he had sucked on her nipple. She cut loose with a shriek which she smothered by placing an arm over her mouth.

His tongue dipped into her honeycomb. Madelyn's thigh closed, holding him there, while her other hand pressed against the back of his head as if to push him up into her. "More! More!"

Obliging, Fargo lapped at her until his tongue was sore. She moaned nonstop, her body pumping to an inner rhythm, adrift in ecstasy.

Fargo's manhood ached for release. Unhitching his gunbelt and his pants, he shoved his pants low enough to free it. Madelyn's eyes were closed and stayed closed even when he removed his mouth and aligned himself. She didn't suspect the moment had come. Lightly placing the swollen tip against her womanhood, Fargo held onto her hips, then rammed up into her.

"Eeeeeeeee!" Madelyn screeched and raised both of them off the bed. Eyelids fluttering, she clung to him as if she were drowning and he was her only hope of being saved. Her fingernails were daggers in his biceps.

Fargo rocked on his knees, pumping like a steam engine, raw pleasure coursing through his veins. Adrift in a sea of sensation, he lost all track of time, all sense of where he was. The danger, the urgency, were momentarily forgotten. He was totally relaxed.

The brunette was in the throes of erotic delirium, thrusting to match his movement, her lips like ripe strawberries, her breasts taut, her nipples erect. She was every man's dream, every man's desire.

Shouts outdoors intruded on Fargo's bliss. Rousing himself, he perked his ears. Someone was upset about something or other but the words were too indistinct for him to understand. Then there was a shot, muted by distance. A lot more yelling took place. Additional shots cracked.

Fargo wasn't worried. Whatever was happening, it wasn't anywhere near Lily's. It didn't involve him or pose a threat.

He shut the noises from his mind so he could enjoy himself that much more.

"Ohhh, don't ever stop," Madelyn mewed. "This is heaven."

Their bodies were slapping together in cadence, her hips fused with his. Fargo kissed those strawberry lips, her mouth melting into his like maple syrup. He sucked on her tongue, and she on his. Lost in their private paradise, they were slow to react to the pounding on the door.

When the knocks registered, Fargo tensed and raised up on his knees. Still joined at the waist, he snatched the Colt and cocked it.

Madelyn, scowling, rose onto her elbows. With a visible effort she controlled her breathing and called out, "Go away! I don't want to be disturbed!"

"Maddy!" a woman with a squeaky voice responded. "It's Claire! Didn't you hear all that shooting?"

"No. And I don't care. Go away. Lily gave me some time to myself."

Claire didn't listen. "Wait until you hear! Word is that One-Eared John is dead! Some of his friends are real upset about it, and they started some trouble."

"Are you hard of hearing? I wouldn't give a lick if those vipers kill themselves off! Now go the hell away and don't bother me again!"

"I only thought you'd want to know," Claire said petulantly.

Fargo waited to be sure she left. The news was of special interest. It might be helpful, if he could find a way to exploit it.

"What are you doing, handsome?" Madelyn asked. "Daydreaming? At a time like this? Finish what we started."

No coaxing was needed. Fargo resumed his stroking. Before long the room and the bed and the ceiling receded into a white haze. There was just the two of them, Madelyn kissing his jaw, his neck, his chest. He cupped a breast, pinching and pulling on it, while his other hand slid under her behind.

"That's it, big man! That's it!" Suddenly Madelyn threw her head back. "Ahhhh! I'm coming! Oh, yes! Yes!" True to her word, her hips windmilled in a frenzy.

Fargo usually liked to last longer. But the shots and the shouts and Claire's interruption had reminded him there was a time and place for everything, and it wouldn't do to be caught with his pants down. He opened the floodgates to the explosion he had been holding back, and once he did, he was swept up by the rip current of his own passion and borne over the brink.

It was marvelous.

# 6

Hender's Gap was as still as a cemetery, but the stillness was deceiving.

Skye Fargo had left Madelyn Mosely in dreamland and climbed out the window. Her two hours were about up, and he'd figured Lily would send someone to fetch her if she didn't show up at the saloon soon. But the saloon was closed and dark, as was the general store and the livery. Only in the hotel and in most of the shacks did lights blaze. It was as if the town had been shut down for the night and everyone had been ordered to turn in.

Fargo had the street all to himself. Or so he assumed until he passed the saloon and the thud of boots alerted him to a knot of men approaching from the south. Flying into the next doorway, he palmed the Colt.

There were five of them, all bearing rifles. In the lead was Hiram, the young bodyguard Ira had put in charge of disposing of One-Eared John's friends. The job apparently done, Hiram was patrolling the town, a swagger to his stride.

A beanpole in a floppy hat marched beside him and was saying, "—winged Caleb thataway! Things are going to hell right quick around here."

"Trust in Uncle Ira," Hiram said. "He's never failed us yet, has he? He'll calm the rowdies down and restore order."

"I hope you're right," the beanpole said doubtfully.

"Some of those fellers are downright wicked. Stirrin' them up is like stirrin' up a beehive."

Fargo retreated as far back as the recessed doorway allowed. Claire's information had been accurate, then. Word of One-Eared John's death had leaked, and now there was bad blood between the Hender clan and the outlaws.

"They're not so tough," Hiram said. "We made them back down, didn't we? They slunk off like curs when Caleb ordered them to clear the street. Nobody'll show their faces until daylight, like they were told."

The beanpole wasn't as confident. "Rabid dogs can't be leash-broke, sonny. They always tear off the hand of the mulehead who tries. And those Texicans are as rabid a bunch as you'll ever meet."

"They don't scare me none."

Inexperience and bluster went hand in hand, Fargo mused. They failed to notice him and were soon out of earshot. Warily, he moved on to the general store. In the belief Sam Hender had gone home for the night, Fargo crept on past it, then stopped when he spied a light at the rear. As noiselessly as a panther he snuck to a window. In a small room, seated at a desk, was the storekeeper, his nose buried in an account book.

A few yards off was a door left ajar to let in the night breeze. The hinges didn't creak as Fargo eased it open. On the tips of his toes he stalked closer and gouged the Colt's barrel into the base of the thin man's neck. "Not one peep or you're dead."

Sam turned to stone. "Who are you? What do you want? If it's money, I don't have any. The day's receipts are always turned over to Ira at closing time."

"Where's the boy?"

"The who?"

Grabbing the chair, Fargo swung it partway around, nearly upending the storekeeper in the process. Sam's left eyelid was twitching worse than ever. "His name is Wes, remember? The boy you claimed that you never saw."

"But I didn't—"

Fargo smashed the revolver against the storekeeper's temple and Sam doubled over in agony. "I overheard Ira. He said you had seen to it the boy would be taken care of. How? What did you do?"

"Honestly, I don't have any idea—"

Again Fargo swung the Colt. This time Sam fell to the floor, onto his hands and knees. "No more lies," Fargo warned. "The truth, and nothing but the truth, or you'll have more busted ribs."

"Ribs?" Sam repeated, befuddled by pain. "My ribs are fine."

"Not anymore," Fargo said, and kicked him in the chest, sinking the tip of his boot in deep. A sharp crack brought a shriek to Sam's lips but he stifled it when the pistol touched the tip of his nose. Bleating pathetically, Sam wheezed as if his lungs were about to collapse.

Fargo flung him against the desk. "We'll try this once more. The boy rode into town looking for his cousin. He stopped at the general store to ask if you had seen her. What did you tell him?"

"I told him no," Sam blubbered.

"But you and I both know you were lying," Fargo bluffed. "Where is she being kept? At the hotel?"

"Only Ira and those with lots of money stay there. Where else would she be but at Lily's Place?"

The revelation stunned Fargo. He had been in the same building, maybe just a few rooms away. Asking why she was there would be pointless. The answer was as plain as the twitch in Sam's left eye.

"Sline brought her, like he does a lot of the gals. The way I hear it, he happened to see her comin' out of a chicken coop as he was ridin' by the Dixon farm. She's prettier than most, so he stopped and dickered with her pa. Turns out, her pa is a drunk and deep in debt. So Sline offered to give the man the money he needed if she would come work here for a year." Sam was babbling, spilling secrets in his fear. "She had no idea what she was being brought here for. Sline told her she would be workin' as a maid for a rich couple."

"This Sline, is he a Hender or a Mosely?"

"Neither. Jacob Sline is the only outsider Ira trusts. They were friends when Ira was a boy, and Ira relies on him in dealin' with the outside world. It's Sline who ships in most of our supplies, brings in women to work at Lily's, and spreads word of our town to the right people."

"To outlaws. To murderers and thieves and anyone else wanted by the law."

Sam forced a grin. "You've got to hand it to my uncle. It's a brilliant scheme. Any ranger who happens by will think Hender's Gap is just another small town full of nice, law-abidin' folks."

"Finish telling me about the boy. What did you do to him? Is he still alive?"

"Do you think I'd do a thing like that?" Sam countered, then cringed when Fargo seized the front of his shirt. "No! Listen, I'll tell you the honest truth. He came into my store and asked if Susie Dixon was a customer of mine. I played dumb and quizzed him. When I realized she was his kin, and that he'd come all this way to find her, I told her she was at a spread east of here. Ira sent a couple of men there to act as our eyes and ears, as it were."

"Theo and Orville Mosely?" Fargo said.

"That's them. But how do you know who they are?"

Fargo was confused. "Why would you send Wes there?" No sooner did he ask the question than the answer occurred to him. Theo and Orville were under orders to slay anyone who was a threat to Ira's empire. That included nosy ten-year-olds.

Sam jerked away. "What's wrong? Why are you lookin' at me like that? I never hurt the kid! On my word of honor!"

"Scum have no honor," Fargo said, glancing around for something to tie the storekeeper up with. Now that every-thing had been explained, one part puzzled him. Wes knew all about Theo and Orville, and would have seen through

Sam's ruse. Yet if Wes hadn't gone back to the ranch, where *had* he gone off to?

Deep in thought, Fargo was a shade slow in defending himself when Sam Hender twisted and heaved the chair at his chest. He swatted it aside, bruising his forearm, then dived as Sam scuttled like a crab for the door. A shot would bring Hiram, so he had to stop the storekeeper without using the Colt. But Sam was no weakling. Wiry as a weasel, he twisted and kicked, eluding Fargo's grasp.

"Help! For God's sake, someone help me!"

Frantically lurching forward, Sam reached the doorway and started to throw himself out. Only Fargo's outflung hand, seizing his ankle, stopped him. But the damage had been done.

From down the street came an answering shout.

Sam kicked savagely, bawling, "Hiram! Jethro! Caleb! Help! Come quick! The back of my store!" He had hold of the jamb and was gripping it violently.

A lunge put Fargo astraddle the storekeeper's legs. In order to make Hender let go, he bashed the man's knuckles. It worked. Howling like a wounded banshee, Sam sprawled onto his stomach. In a blink of an eye Fargo struck again, not once but twice, slugging Sam across the back of the head.

As the storekeeper went limp, Fargo jumped to the lamp and blew it out, shrouding the room in darkness. But was it soon enough? Rushing to the doorway, he listened to the drum of feet. Figures materialized at the alley's mouth.

"I thought it came from Sam's place but all his lights are out." That was Hiram.

"Maybe it was further down."

"I couldn't quite make out what they were sayin'," commented a third man. "All I caught was 'help.'"

"We'll divide up," Hiram said. "Chester, you and Billy go down the other side and we'll take this side. If you see anything suspicious, anything at all, give a holler and we'll come runnin'."

"Will do."

They disappeared. Safe for the time being, Fargo scoured the room and found a folded blanket on a shelf. Using the Arkansas toothpick, he cut it into strips with which he bound and gagged Sam Hender. To hinder anyone from finding him any time soon, Fargo bolted the door from the inside and climbed out the window.

Rather than head for the street, Fargo hastened to the back of the general store and turned to the right. To reach the livery he had to pass a row of shacks and one sorry excuse for a house. In most of the buildings lights gleamed from the windows. As silently as a Sioux warrior he glided past them. In one, a man and woman were arguing, in another two children giggled and squealed, from a third issued moans and the creek of bedsprings.

At the last shack, Fargo halted. The livery was still lit up, its great doors open wide. To go in the front invited discovery, so Fargo sprinted toward the north wall. He wasn't quite halfway there when two men walked out. It was Hiram and the beanpole. Diving flat, Fargo braced for an outcry but they hadn't seen him. They were too busy bickering.

"I'm telling you," the beanpole said, "we should go door-to-door. Someone needs our help and it's our job to find out who."

Hiram disagreed. "Bother everyone at this time of night? Maybe wake some of them up? What if they complain to Ira? I'd rather kiss a coiled sidewinder than have him mad at me."

"What if tomorrow they find someone dead? And what if Ira learns we heard a cry for help but never caught who did the killin'? How do you reckon he'll take that? With a smile and a clap on the back for a job well done?"

"You have a point," Hiram conceded.

"Better safe than breathin' dirt is my motto," the beanpole stated. "He can't accuse us of slackin' off if we've done all we can."

Cursing like a muleskinner, Hiram headed on up the street, the beanpole in tow.

Fargo rose and broke into a headlong spring. Melting into black shadows, he ran to the rear. A small corral held a handful of horses of no special interest. He tested the latch on a door, then slipped inside. On the right were bales of hay, on the left was a high mound of straw.

Acting on a hunch, Fargo inspected the stalls. He felt certain the Ovaro would be there but it wasn't. Disappointed, he was mulling over his options when a rustling noise brought him around in a streak of buckskin, the Colt clearing leather.

A brown hat too big for the head it was on rose from the straw. Under it was a youthful face creased by a grin. John Wesley stood, a derringer in either hand. "You're back! With all the shooting and shouting, I thought you were a goner."

"They're trying their best to bring me to bay," Fargo replied. Then it hit him what the boy had said. "Wait a minute. Were you there when I came in earlier looking for you?"

Wes nodded as he stepped from the pile. "Sure. But I couldn't very well say anything with the liveryman dimwit here, now could I?" Wes began brushing bits of straw from his shirt and pants. "The first stop I made when I got to town was at the general store. When the man there told me Susie was staying with those two jackasses who tried to make worm food of us, Theo and Orville, I figured something was real wrong. He had to be in on it. And if he was, so were others. I couldn't trust anyone."

"Not even me?"

"I saw your pinto in front of the saloon and was about to go there when I spotted the fat marshal heading for the store. When he turned to talk to a lady, I led the mare around back, then came here. The liveryman was busy with a customer so he never caught me putting the mare in the corral. I've been hiding ever since, waiting for nightfall."

Fargo was impressed. The boy had handled himself as smartly as any adult.

"I would've come out of hiding sooner. But with all the ruckus, I didn't think it was safe." Wes wedged the derringers under his belt. "What were you just searching for? Your pinto? It's not here. A man named Sline took it."

There was that name again. "How do you know?" Fargo asked.

Wes pointed at a dun in the last stall. "There's his horse. Shortly after I snuck in here, he showed up and told the liveryman to saddle it. About that time, that hog of a lawman waddled in leading your stallion. The lawdog told Sline to take it, no questions asked, and light a shuck out of town. Sline said he was headed home anyway." Wes paused. "From what I gather, he has a place west of here."

No wonder Fargo couldn't find the Ovaro anyway. Crafty Caleb had seen to it he couldn't leave town unless he stole someone else's mount. Which would give Caleb a legal excuse to hunt him down and slay him—not that the lawman needed one.

A saddle and blanket on the stall beside the dun had to be Sline's. Fargo went over and helped himself to them.

"Hold on," Wes said. "Susie is more important than any dumb horse. Help me find her and I'll help you get your animal back."

"You heard all the commotion," Fargo said. "Hender's Gap is sealed up tighter than a miser's fist. We'd be caught. And then who would save your cousin? No, we wait and come back tomorrow night. By then it should be safe."

"Wait another whole day?" Wes wasn't happy. "I guess you're right. But it galls me, all this slinking around. When I'm a man, I'll never run from trouble. No matter what."

Fargo opened the stall and patted the dun so it wouldn't be skittish. "In the meantime, I want a few words with Jacob Sline." He truly did. Plus, he wanted to get the boy out of there, to somewhere safe.

"You're not the only one." Wes hustled toward the back door. "I'll be ready to go quicker than you can count two."

Fargo finished saddling up, snuffed out the lantern, and swung onto the dun's hurricane deck. The street appeared empty. But as Fargo rode through the great doors, a clamor at the rear of the general store warned him it wouldn't be for long. They had found Sam Hender.

Wes was waiting at the corral. Side by side they trotted into the high grass and presently were out of rifle range. Fargo was glad to be shed of the hellhole, if only for a while. It went against his grain to leave Susan Dixon behind, but they couldn't spirit her out of there with the situation as it was. She was safe enough at Lily's.

Locating Jacob Sline's place wasn't much of a challenge. A pinpoint of light among the foremost hills led them to a large cabin, part wood, part stone, part sod. Fargo and Wes gave it a wide berth and climbed to a ridge overlooking the site. From their vantage point they saw that a horseshoe-shaped ridge flanked the cabin on three sides. The only approach was from the front. A log pen at the rear held a horse and a mule.

"Yonder is your pinto," Wes commented.

Finding the Ovaro was one thing, reclaiming it another. Sline had built the pen so that no one could get to the gate without going past the cabin, unless they were a mountain goat. A prudent precaution in Comanche country.

Wes drew a derringer. "Stay here until I'm done with him."

"Hold it." Fargo snagged the youngster's shirt. "Where do you think you're going?"

"Jacob Sline was the one who took Susie. He has a lot to answer for." To accent his point, Wes sighted down the derringer. "She's my blood kin so this is mine to do." As nonchalantly as if he were on a Sunday stroll, the boy started down the slope.

Fargo was beginning to appreciate why parents had gray hair before they were forty. "You're the one who will stay here," he directed, and pulled the youngster back up. "I need Sline alive to answer a few questions."

"Aw, shucks. You're worse than my pa."

Fargo descended rapidly. A belt of brush afforded the cover he needed to come within a stone's throw of the front door. Light shone through a small window to the right and Fargo noticed a shadow flitting past it like a raven. There was a sound, like two hands smacking together, or a slap. Fargo couldn't be sure.

Breaking from concealment, Fargo darted toward the nearest corner. An ominous growl brought him to a halt. From out of the murkiness padded a large black dog, a mongrel as big as a small bear. The hackles on its neck were up and its fangs were bared.

Fargo could shoot it, but that would alert Sline. Spinning, he raced for the brush. The dog barked, then charged, loping at incredible speed. It was nipping at his heels when all of a sudden it yelped and was flung onto its back as if by an invisible hand. A long rope tied to a stake in front of the cabin had spared Fargo. He gained the thicket and hunkered low as the door opened.

"What in the hell are you barkin' about now, Andy?" asked a seemingly frail man with shoulder-length white hair and a cane. He surveyed the ridge, then shook his cane at the dog. "Another damn rabbit, I'll wager. When will you learn?"

The black dog was on its feet, legs stiff, growling at the brush.

"I'm sick and tired of this nonsense," Jacob Sline said. "You're supposed to bark if a rider comes, or if you sniff an Injun. Not every time a bunny hops by."

Thanks to the wind, which was blowing Fargo's scent toward them, the dog had him pinpointed. It stared right at him, bristling from head to tail.

"You sure don't listen, do you, Andy?" Sline said, and with surprising alacrity he sharply struck the mongrel's back with the cane. The dog yipped, slinking aside as Sline hit it over and over, pummeling it into submission. Only when Andy ran to the left side of the cabin and lay with his head on his paws did Sline's wrath subside.

"No more infernal barkin'!" Sline raged, shaking the cane. "I shoot dogs that don't earn their keep, and you're dangerously close to not earnin' yours."

The door slammed. Andy whined a few times and was still.

Fargo sidled to the right in a wide loop to come up on the cabin from the rear. Picking a path down the slope required patience. At the bottom he stole to the log rails and was greeted by the Ovaro. No windows were at the back so he could take the pinto and go. Except for one thing. His saddle, saddle blanket, and saddlebags had to be inside. To say nothing of the Henry.

Fargo roved along the pen to the north wall and on to the front corner. The dog was on the other side so he should be safe enough, provided it didn't hear him. He glanced up at the ridge but didn't see any sign of Wes.

Inside the cabin a loud thump resounded. Through the window drifted Sline's voice, grating like sand on tin.

"You're more stubborn than most, I'll grant you that much. But you're only delayin' the outcome. I always have my way. Always."

Curious to learn whom the man was talking to, Fargo slunk toward the window. He kept one eye on the opposite corner in case Andy showed. Suddenly the light was almost blotted out.

Jacob Sline was gazing down at the distant lights of Hender's Gap. "You were probably wonderin' why I live up here all alone instead of in town with everyone else. Now you know. Down there, all the screamin' and whatnot would attract too much attention. Even Ira couldn't protect me if the truth were known."

Fargo saw Sline's fingers curl around the bottom sill.

"Ironic, isn't it, my dear? Some of the wickedest killers ever to walk this earth would string me up by my heels and gut me if they learned what I do. Ira looks the other way, but only because he needs me. I'm his link to the outside world, the one person he can't do without."

Someone—a woman—answered, but Fargo couldn't hear what she said.

"Why? Haven't you guessed by now?" Sline said. "It's my pet passion. I couldn't live without it even if I wanted to, and I don't want to. How did I get started? When I was eleven. But I'll spare you the details. I'm not here to entertain you. You're here to entertain me, and so far you've been doing a poor job."

Fargo heard her next remark plainly.

"You're a beast, Sline! A despicable beast!"

The white-haired man laughed. "I know I am, woman. And I make no apologies for my nature. So what's next? Will you plead? Will you rave? Will you do as so many do and waste your breath insultin' me?"

"No," the woman said. "But I want you to know I hate you."

"Good. You should. I tore you from hearth and home and brought you here under false pretenses. If you claimed that you didn't despise me, I would say you're a liar." Sline's fingers uncurled and he turned. "Enough pleasant chat. We'll begin anew. And before I'm done, you'll lick my feet and love it."

"Never!"

The light was blotted out completely. Craning his neck, Fargo saw that a strip of blanket serving as curtain had been pulled across the window. Jerking the Colt, he moved to the door.

"Don't you dare come near me! I swear, I'll rip your eyes out!"

The hinges creaked but the woman's anxious shout eclipsed it. Fargo took a step inside, not knowing what to expect but certainly not expecting what he found. Facing the far wall was a naked woman, chained to shackles imbedded in the logs. She had been brutally whipped, her back a maze of cuts and gashes. On the right wall was another woman, so thin she was a broomstick, her body a wreck.

In the center of the room stood Jacob Sline. He had traded the cane for a bullwhip and was slowly uncoiling it. "I think I'll peel your skin off an inch at a time, starting at your neck and working my way down."

"Quit crowing and do it. I haven't cried out yet and I'm not about to."

Sline flicked the whip so the tip cracked like a gunshot close to her ear. "My dear Elsie, you haven't felt anything yet. I've only just begin."

Fargo curled back the Colt's hammer. "That's where you're wrong, mister. It's over. You're setting her free."

The white-haired man bestowed a demonic smile over a sloped shoulder. "Well, well, well. What have we here? A knight errant in buckskins? Whoever you are, I'll give you five seconds to drop your six-shooter."

"You've got it backwards, don't you?" Fargo said. The man was in no position to make demands, not when he was staring down the barrel of a cocked revolver. Then Jacob Sline smiled, and Fargo knew why Sline wasn't worried. He knew it before a rumbling snarl filled the cabin and the red-head screamed.

"Look out! His dog will tear you apart!"

# 7

Skye Fargo had heard it said that a man should always choose the lesser of two evils. But these threats to his life were equally deadly. A bullwhip in the hands of a master was a formidable weapon, while the dog's ferocity spoke for itself.

With only a split second to decide, Fargo elected to whirl toward the mongrel. It was closer than Jacob Sline and its tapered teeth could rip his legs to shreds in the time it took Sline to swing the whip. Fargo skipped backward as he turned away from the door, only a footstep or two ahead of the black dog, which hurled itself at him like a wolverine gone berserk. Slavering and snapping, it nearly sheared into his shin.

Fargo extended the Colt. Before he could shoot, the bullwhip wrapped around his wrist, stinging terribly. His arm was yanked so hard the pistol was torn from his grasp. Fargo had to dig his heels in to keep from being pulled off balance. He clawed at the lash to unwind it, and as he did so, razor-sharp teeth seared into his lower leg. Desperately, he threw himself to the left to evade the dog's slashing fangs.

Andy surged forward, not to be denied. But just when his jaws were swooping at Fargo's ankle, he was brought to a lurching stop. The dog had come to the end of the rope. Barking and biting, he frenziedly sought to sink his teeth into Fargo again but he couldn't quite reach.

Fargo had a problem of his own. Jacob Sline was tugging on the bullwhip and swinging it from side to side to prevent him from unwinding the rawhide. Again and again Fargo tried to hold still, but Sline always darted to the left or the right, nearly pulling him off his feet. Fargo was vaguely aware of the redhead, aghast at his plight.

"Kill him, Andy! Kill him, boy!" Sline screamed.

The mongrel was doing its utmost to obey. It leaped and barked and thrashed in a bid to escape the rope, beside itself with unbridled fury.

Sline suddenly slanted toward the dog, the whip taut so Fargo couldn't loosen it. His intent was transparent. He wanted to haul Fargo within reach of those fearsome jaws, and that would be that.

Fargo bent to try and reach the Arkansas toothpick but the whip hindered him. He couldn't bend far enough. Nor could he back away any further. Yet he had to do something, and do it swiftly, or he would be at their mercy. The tension on the whip was the key. Sline's ploy would work only as long as Fargo continued to resist.

But what if he didn't? Fargo launched himself at the pair, pretending to charge Sline. At the last moment, as the mongrel leaped to intercept him, he sidestepped, holding his arm so the dog's razor teeth sliced into the whip instead of his wrist.

"No!" Sline cried in a rage.

The bullwhip was completely severed. Andy landed awkwardly and slipped but was immediately upright.

Fargo vaulted toward the Colt, retrieving it as Sline stooped to untie the dog. "I'd think twice, if I were you."

The white-haired man froze. Up close, he didn't appear old at all. His hair must have gone prematurely white because he couldn't be more than forty.

"Drop the whip," Fargo instructed him. "Then shove your dog outside and close the door."

"Are you that eager to fill a hole in the ground?" Sline responded. "I work for a man who has a small army at his beck and call. He won't take kindly to this. My advice to you, stranger, is to holster that hogleg and leave. Forget what you've seen here and you'll be better off."

"The dog," Fargo demanded.

Sullenly, Sline dropped the bullwhip and gripped Andy's collar. The mongrel fought him, snapping and scrabbling in a bid to reach Fargo. Sline had to smack it several times to get it to heed. He virtually threw it over the threshold and slammed the door in its ferocious face. But it clawed to get back in, howling like a wolf. "There," Sline taunted. "Satisfied?"

"No. Release the women."

Elsie had sagged against the wall, her eyes brimming with tears. "I can't believe the nightmare is really over," she said with a sob. "Thank God! I'm forever in your debt. What's your name? Where did you come from?"

The answers had to wait. Fargo didn't trust Sline any further than he could heave the cabin. He watched carefully as Ira's lieutenant limped to a wall and removed a large key from a wooden peg. "No tricks."

Sline inserted the key into the right lock.

The redhead was so weak that when the shackle opened she pitched to one side. Suspended by her other arm, which bore her whole weight, she grimaced but didn't utter a sound. Rising, she rested her forehead against the logs and steadied herself.

Sline rotated toward the second shackle. "Ever heard of Ira Hender, stranger? He's a big man in these parts. He runs that town down in the valley. And if anything happens to me, you'll answer to him."

"I hear that Ira and you grew up together," Fargo mentioned.

"You've met him?" Sline smirked. "Then you know I'm not exaggeratin' when I say he's the next best thing to the Almighty in these parts. Skedaddle now, and I'm willing to chalk this whole thing up to a misunderstandin'."

"You're all heart."

Sline stuck the key into the lock. "Sticks and stones, mister. Sticks and stones." He twisted the key. "Yes, Ira and I have been pards since we weren't much taller than a well pump. We drifted apart when my parents drug me to Ohio for a couple of years. But we got back together later, and I've been at his side ever since. He knows the value of a friend."

"But not of human life." Fargo moved to the left so he would have a clear shot should the need arise.

"You can't blame this on him," Sline said, nodding at Elsie and the other woman, who hadn't moved since Fargo entered. "It's a private indulgence. Ira has a few of his own."

The redhead suddenly tottered. She was free but she could barely stand. Her wrists were rubbed raw, fresh blood matting her arms. Clenching her fists, she weakly swung at her tormentor but couldn't connect.

Jacob Sline chuckled. "A word of advice, my dear. I would take you much more seriously if you had clothes on."

"You—you—!" Elsie couldn't find words fitting enough. Staggering to the only chair in the room, she sat, primly crossing her legs and making a halfhearted attempt to cover her breasts.

Fargo motioned at the other woman. "Set her free, too."

"No need. She died on me this morning and I haven't gotten around to buryin' her yet. I was puttin' it off until tomorrow."

It was true. Fargo felt for a pulse but there was none. Her hair hid her open eyes, which mirrored the anguish and fright she had felt at the moment of her death. Something inside of Fargo snapped as he stared into them. "Toss the key."

Sline did so.

"Now face the wall and shackle your left wrist."

"If you insist. But you really should get out of here and take sweet Elsie with you while you still can. I'm expecting a messenger from Ira any time now." Realizing the threat had no effect, Sline reluctantly complied and slid his wrist into the heavy shackle. It locked with a loud snap. "Now what? As if I can't guess."

"Face the wall." Fargo rammed the barrel into the man's backbone and held it there while applying the other shackle. Done, he twirled the Colt into his holster.

"Giving me a taste of my own medicine, is that it?" Sline said. "Have your fun while you can, stranger. Before another day is out you'll be buzzard bait. I guarantee it."

All this while Andy had been tearing at the door in a paroxysm of bestial rage. Fargo was glad when the dog desisted, until he realized why.

"Out of my way, you stupid critter!"

*Wes!* Fargo sprang for the door as a piercing yowl rent the night. The mongrel had attacked! Simultaneously, a derringer cracked, then another. Flinging the door open, Fargo saw the dog tumble to rest in a disjointed, miserable heap.

John Wesley sauntered past it as if slaying vicious beasts was a daily ritual. "I got tired of waiting," the boy said. "Are you finished with Sline yet?" He came in and almost tripped over his own feet in astonishment. Blinking at the dead woman and the redhead, he blurted, "Dog my cats!"

Lying on a counter was a long black coat, which Fargo retrieved and draped over Elsie's slim shoulders. She was shivering, but not from being cold. In a cupboard he found a loaf of moldy bread and venison jerky. "You need to eat," he said kindly, placing both in her hands. "To build up your strength." She nibbled at the bread.

"What's wrong with her?" Wes asked.

"She's been through hell." Fargo left it at that. With any luck, in time she would banish the memories and recover. Nightmares might afflict her for the rest of her life, but at least she *was* alive. "Take her outside."

"But I wanted to—" the boy began, looking from Elsie to Jacob Sline. "Oh, all right." A shade nervously, he clasped her arm. "Did you hear him, ma'am? Let's get you some fresh air."

Elsie absently nodded. "That would be nice, yes. I haven't

been out of this horrid cabin in over a week. Thank you, young man."

Fargo spotted his saddle and personal effects in a corner. Replacing the key on the peg, he gathered his belongings. The Henry had been left in the scabbard and his saddlebags contained all the items they should. As he slung the saddle over a shoulder, Jacob Sline rattled the chains.

"What are you fixin' to do, mister?"

Making no answer, Fargo headed for the entrance.

"Do you aim to turn me over to the law? Is that it? What if I made it worth your while not to? I have some money squirreled away, most of what Ira has paid me, and it's yours if you'll give me the key and just go."

Fargo had met some blackhearted bastards in his travels but few rivaled this fiend in the cabin. Ira Hender did. The two were a matched set, like bookends or pistols. Judging which was worse was impossible. Both were blights on everything decent people considered good and true and right. And while Fargo didn't consider himself a paragon of virtue, as a minister might say, he couldn't let this kind of blight spread. Enough innocents had already suffered. It had to end.

The Ovaro stomped and bobbed its head, eager to stretch its legs. But after Fargo saddled it, he brought both animals around front and tied the pinto and mule to bushes near where Elsie sat munching on venison.

Wes was hovering over her as if she were his mother. "This poor lady's in a bad way," he whispered. "I can't hardly get two words out of her."

"She's had a rough time of it." Fargo gave the Henry to him. "Hold on to this. There's one last thing I need to do."

"What about Sline? You're not letting him get away with what he's done, are you? No one should mistreat women. Ever."

"Trust me. You'll like what I have in mind."

The fireplace hadn't been used recently. In a pot on a tripod was cold stew, and the charred firewood under it wouldn't do. But deeper down, under the burnt limbs, and under a layer of ash and soot, Fargo uncovered an ember warm enough for his purpose. Leaving it there, he gathered an armful of clothes, blankets, and bedding. These, he deposited in the middle of the floor, topping the pile with the makeshift curtain.

Jacob Sline watched uneasily. When Fargo returned to the fireplace, he couldn't remain silent any longer. "What the hell are you doing? Why did you dump all that stuff there?"

A poker and a stick were sufficient for Fargo to lift the center from the ash and bear it to the pile.

Sline stepped from the wall as far as the chains allowed. "Hold on. You're not setting that on fire, are you? What's to stop my cabin from burning to the ground?"

"Nothing," Fargo said. He blew lightly on the ember.

"Damn you! You expect me to stand out there and watch my place go up in smoke? Is that your notion of punishment?"

"No, you'll be inside."

The significance was slow to sink in. When it did, Sline chortled as if Fargo had jested. But when Fargo kept on blowing on the ember, Sline's expression changed from amused to one of disbelief. "I can't be hearin' right. I could have sworn you just said I'd be in here when the cabin goes up."

"You will be."

"That's murder!" Sline declared, throwing himself against the shackles.

"And what do you call what you did to her?" Fargo tilted his head at the dead woman. The ember was starting to glow. Soon it would be red-hot.

"Yes, yes, but—" Sline stopped as it dawned that no argument would justify her suffering. So he grasped at a different straw. "Listen, this is the same as lynch law. As stringin' a man up without a trial. Don't I deserve that much? You should turn me over to the Texas Rangers or a sheriff somewhere and have them throw me behind bars."

Fargo's exhaled, inhaled, exhaled. "That would take days, maybe a week. I don't have the time to spare. The boy and I came to Hender's Gap for Susan Dixon and we're not leaving without her."

"I can help you! I can go anywhere in town, no questions asked. I'll ride in and fetch her for you if you'll give me your word to let me go when she's safe. How about it? Do we have a deal?"

"We'll get her out without your help." Fargo squatted. Another few times should do it. The pile would ignite rapidly, spreading to the roof and from there to all four walls, consuming the dry logs as if they were so much paper.

"Not without bloodshed," Sline said. Gnawing his lower lip, he gazed hopelessly around the room, craving salvation that wasn't there. "Dixon or the boy might wind up hurt. Do you want that on your conscience?"

"What do you know about conscience?" Fargo rejoined. The ember now blazed scarlet. Lowering it onto an old blanket, he straightened as tiny wisps of smoke curled upward. Soon, miniature flames formed a ring that spread and grew. Standing, he gave the dead woman a last glance. He'd rather bury her, but if they were to reach Hender's Gap well before dawn, they couldn't dally.

"Don't do this!" Sline pleaded. "Being burned alive is a rotten way to die!"

"Is there ever a good way?" Having had enough of the man, Fargo walked to the door. Flames six inches high were climbing the pile, leaping from garment to garment like mountain sheep vaulting from ledge to ledge.

"Wait!" Sline screeched, fear oozing from every pore. "Aren't you interested in that money I told you about? Over six hundred dollars, all yours! It's buried out back! Undo these shackles and I'll show you where! Hell, I'll even dig it up for you!"

Fargo saw a finger of fire scale the top and lick toward the ceiling. It wasn't high enough—yet. "How many women are buried out back with that money?" he asked.

Anger surfaced and Sline shook the chains. "Release me! Now! This has gone far enough!"

The heat was rising. The clothes were fully aflame, crackling and hissing, red and orange tips spearing higher, ever higher. Fargo took a step backward, blocking the doorway so Elsie couldn't see.

Jacob Sline's wide eyes fixed on the pile. "No!" he roared like a grizzly. "I won't let this happen! I won't!" Placing his hands flat against the wall, he pushed off with his arms and legs, heaving outward, seeking to rip the shackles loose. But the same hard iron that had held so many helpless women now did the same to him.

A breezy gust from outside fanned the fire. Hungry flames scorched the ceiling. A log sizzled and sputtered and then burst into flame.

"Adios," Fargo said, tapping his hat brim. He moved toward the horse, halting when a strident scream quavered from the throat of a man at sanity's brink. Sline was beside himself, tugging and kicking and pushing, doing all in his power to stave off his doom. "Now you know how those women felt," Fargo said.

A short finger materialized at his elbow. "An eye for an eye. I like that."

Flames danced across the ceiling with astounding speed. The cabin was a giant tinderbox and everything in it so much kindling. Sline stopped wrenching on the chains to gape in horror at the growing inferno. He watched, mesmerized, as fire ate its way toward the wall he was shackled to. "Help! Help me! For God's sake, don't let me die like this!"

"No grit," Wes commented. "When my time comes, I want to meet my Maker like a man ought to. Not bawling like a baby."

"You shouldn't see this," Fargo said. "You're too young."

"Do you think I haven't seen people die before? In my neck of the woods, folks are always feuding, always killing each other off. When I was five I saw an uncle who had been shot so full of holes, he looked like a sieve."

Jacob Sline vented a shrill shriek and renewed his assault on the chains. Smoke was filling the room, and he coughed and hacked as he desperately, madly, sought to preserve his life. A line of flame reached the top of his wall and licked lower.

Fargo started to turn. "Let's go. We don't need to watch this."

"You're wrong, mister. I do." Unnoticed by either of them, Elsie had come over. She was transfixed by the tableau. A peculiar gleam lit her eyes, and she wore an unnerving little smile. "I need to see him get what he deserves."

"Haven't you been through enough?" Fargo asked.

"That's just it." The redhead pulled the coat tighter around her body. "The awful things he did to me, to that other girl. Evil things. I can't even talk about them." She clasped her hands as if to pray. "Lord help me, but I want him dead so much, you can't imagine. He's depraved. He doesn't deserve the gift of life." Sline shrieked again, and Elsie's smile broadened. "Such a sweet sound! Did you hear it? Like chimes tinkling in the wind."

Wes, perplexed, looked to Fargo, who placed a hand on the woman's arm. "We don't have a saddle for the mule. Can you ride bareback? If not, there's a mare you can use."

Elsie shrugged his hand off, then seemed to regret doing so. "I appreciate your concern, mister. But I'm fine. Honest. And feeling better every second." She laughed as a third shriek keened.

So much smoke filled the cabin, it was hard to make Sline out. Swirling gray tendrils writhed as if alive, intertwining like snakes, probing, reaching. Another gust of wind parted the coils enough to show Sline still hauling on the chains. He was tiring. And blubbering and weeping uncontrollably.

"That other woman cried, too," Elsie muttered. "She begged him not to hurt her. She pleaded and pleaded. And do you know what he did? He hurt her worse. Almost as if her pleading excited him." Elsie shuddered. "The sad thing is, I never learned her name. She was there when Sline brought me, so weak she could hardly lift her head."

Sline howled like a rabid dog. Swiveling, he spied them, and some of his spite and bluster resurfaced. "Enjoyin' the show? You miserable wretches! I hope Ira gets his hands on you! I hope he has you chopped to bits and fed to the coyotes! I hope—" A billowy cloud of smoke swallowed him, and he wheezed and coughed.

Elsie giggled. "Isn't that a sight for sore eyes? How long before the roof caves in, you reckon? Won't that be glorious!"

Fargo had no hankering to witness the outcome. Yet, what could he do short of throw her over his shoulder and cart her off against her will? Wes was staring at the redhead in amazement. Maybe it had never occurred to the boy that women could be as spiteful as men. More so, at times.

A great roaring rose louder and louder, punctuated by crackling and sizzling and sharp pops. Scorching waves of heat rippled from the doorway. Jacob Sline wailed and ranted between choking sobs and fits of hacking as smoke filled the cabin.

"I can't see him anymore," Elsie complained.

Flames appeared above the cabin, mushrooming as the night air fueled them. From the window gushed a fiery tongue that flicked toward Fargo and the others, forcing them back. Fargo grabbed the redhead and pulled her with him so she wouldn't be singed. She was too entranced by the spectacle to save herself.

Fargo walked to the animals. They didn't like the din and the heat, so he turned them so they faced the slope. About then, the derringer-toting hellion joined them.

"Why aren't you watching it burn?"

"Why aren't you?" A convenient flat spot a few feet up the slope was an ideal roost. Fargo sat and leaned back. Although they were fifty feet from the conflagration, it was hot enough to melt butter.

Wes sat down in the same manner and said, "They're

bound to see the fire down in the town. Aren't you worried they'll send some men to check?"

"I'm counting on it," Fargo said. There would be that many fewer gunmen to deal with when he went after Susan Dixon.

"You have it all thought out, don't you?" Wes complimented him. "I'm beginning to take a shine to you, mister. You're a lot different than my pa, but you'd do to ride the river with."

In Texas cow country that was the supreme compliment. Coming from a boy no bigger than a calf, it was humorous. But Fargo didn't insult him by laughing.

"What's your creed, Mr. Fargo?"

"Creed?"

"The code you live by. My pa says every man should have one. His is Scripture. He lives and breathes the Holy Book. But that's not for me. When someone hits me, I can't turn the other cheek. It's just not in me."

"I don't have a code that I know of," Fargo said. "Unless you mean respecting everyone as long as they respect me." Fire was engulfing the front wall. "No one can lay a hand on me. Or insult me. And I always try to talk with a straight tongue, as the Sioux say."

"We're a lot alike," Wes remarked.

Fargo disagreed. The youngster was much too ready to kill, too quick to resort to a gun to settle disputes. Later in life it would get him into a lot of trouble if he wasn't careful. Those who lived by the gun usually died by it.

Elsie suddenly clapped her hands and squealed in delight. "Oh! Look! Isn't it wonderful! Isn't it grand!"

Roaring flames completely mantled the cabin. Fire shot high into the sky, smoke gushing heavenward to blot out the stars. Logs were cracking like dry brush under the intense heat, and several fell from the ceiling with resounding booms.

"That lady scares me some," Wes whispered. "She's not right in the head."

A minute later the whole roof crashed in. Any chance of Jacob Sline clinging to life was eliminated when tons of burning logs fell, crushing everything beneath.

Tittering, Elsie did a merry jig, then pranced to the slope and beckoned to them. "He's gone. Wasn't it beautiful? We can leave. I'm ready now."

"To do what, ma'am?" Wes replied.

"Why, what else? To kill Ira Hender."

# 8

"It looks quiet enough," John Wesley said.

Almost all the lights in Hender's Gap were out and the town appeared to be slumbering peacefully under the pale starlight. Two windows at Lily's Place and several at the hotel were the only ones lit.

A quarter of a mile was too far for Fargo to tell if Hiram's bunch were still on patrol. He took it for granted they were, knowing Ira Hender wasn't the kind of man to take undue chances.

Rising in the stirrups, Fargo scoured the valley to the west. Half an hour ago, as they made their way through the high grass, a large number of horsemen had galloped out of town toward Sline's. There had been enough forewarning for the three of them to dismount and cover their mounts' muzzles until the cutthroats were gone. It would be another hour before the riders reached the ridge. Plenty of time, Fargo believed.

Elsie pointed at the Hender Hotel. "Well, what are we waiting for? There's the den of the creature we've come to kill. Let's get it over with."

Fargo wished she would listen to reason and not tag along. He'd pretty near talked himself hoarse seeking to convince her it was for the best, to no avail. Her hatred of Ira Hender was nearly as great as her hatred of Sline. Bundled in the long black coat, only her pale face and disheveled hair showing, she was like some ghostly specter of vengeance.

"Give me a gun," Elsie requested.

"I don't have one to spare," Fargo hedged, hoping it would deter her. She would only get herself killed.

Wes piped up, "I do, ma'am. You can have one of mine. But don't forget. It only holds four shots and it's only good at close range."

Elsie fondled the derringer, her twisted smile eerie. "This will do just fine, young man. As the saying goes, the bigger they are, the harder they fall. When I bring Ira down, folks in Missouri will hear it."

"Is that where you're from?" Wes asked.

Fargo was curious, too. She had shared no information about who she was or how she had wound up at Sline's.

"Joplin," Elsie confirmed. "I was teaching school there. One day Jacob Sline rode into town and offered me a position teaching in Hender's Gap for fifty more dollars a month than I was making. And only half as many children. Like an idiot, I accepted." She stuck the derringer in a pocket. "Money makes us do crazy things, son. My intuition told me not to trust him but I didn't listen. And now I'm soiled beyond redemption."

"How so, ma'am?"

"Never you mind. You're too young. Some of what life inflicts on us shouldn't be learned until we're old enough to deal with it, or never at all." Elsie nudged the mule alongside the Ovaro. "And you can quit fretting over me. I'll be fine."

Fargo tried once more. "Sline wasn't boasting. Ira Hender does have a small army at his beck and call. Men who won't hesitate to kill a woman. Or a boy," he added for Wes's benefit.

"You think I don't know that?" Elsie chittered like a riled squirrel. "Sline brought me to that creature to show me off before he tied me up and took me to his cabin. Apparently I was part of Sline's payment for a job well done. Instead of money, Hender sometimes gave him women to do with as he pleased."

"Sline is gone. That should be enough for you."

Elsie leaned over and rested her hand on top of his. "Please. For my own peace of mind I have to see this through. I need to know Hender is dead. I need to see him die with my own eyes. Or I'll never be whole again." She squeezed. "Please."

"Let her come." Wes added his two pesos worth. "We'll protect her from harm."

They were greener than grass, Fargo mused. "Both of you stay behind me. And do as I say at all times. Agreed?" The redhead and the hellion nodded but Fargo had grave reservations. Pricking the Ovaro with his spurs, he trotted to within an arrow's flight of the benighted buildings, then reined up, grounding the pinto. "From here on, we go on foot," he whispered. He yanked the Henry from the saddle scabbard and levered a round into the chamber.

Even in the darkness Wes's excitement was obvious. Fargo wondered whether it was due to the danger facing them or the prospect of putting more holes into people. He steered them to a cluster of shacks north of the hotel. Not so much as a cat stirred. No dogs barked. No challenges were flung from the shadows.

"Talk about a cinch," Wes joked.

Fargo glared at him. "Not a chirp, you hear me?" Bearing to the left, he managed a dozen feet before the next problem presented itself. Elsie gripped his wrist and moved to bar his way.

"What do you think you're doing? Where are you going?" she demanded, gesturing at the hotel. "Ira Hender is there. He never, ever leaves it, according to Sline. And right now he'll be sound asleep, easy pickings."

"First we save Wes's cousin." Fargo regretted he'd neglected to explain the situation on their way in. "She's at Lily's Place. Once she's safe and sound, the two of us will come back to deal with Ira."

"No," Elsie said harshly. "We run too much risk of being seen. Hender will order the whole town out to hunt us. And he'll call all his bodyguards to the hotel. We'll never get close enough to end his reign of terror."

"It's a risk we have to take," Fargo said. Assuming she would follow, he continued on. But in another few feet his wrist was seized again, only this time by Wes.

"Look!"

Shoulders squared, long coat dragging, Elsie had hastened to the south, toward the Hender Hotel.

Fargo was mad enough to chew stones. "Damn! I'll get her." Conscious that at any second Hiram's men or others might appear, he jogged to overtake her. She heard him and ran, her black coat flapping like raven's wings. "Elsie!" he whispered, but was ignored. She raced around a cabin, out of sight.

Streaking toward it, Fargo saw her barreling for the hotel, right out in the open, as bold as brass. He glanced back to motion to Wes to stay where he was, and was flabbergasted to see the boy hurrying toward Lily's. Neither of them had listened! All Elsie cared about was vengeance, all Wes cared about was his kin. Nothing short of dying would stop either of them. Now he was faced with an impossible decision. Whom should he go after? The woman, or the boy? Whomever it was, the other might be dead before he could reach them. In effect, he had to choose which one deserved to live more than the other.

Storm clouds roiling on his brow, Fargo rotated and chased after Wes. Elsie was a grown woman. Her mistakes fell on her own shoulders. Wes, for all his maturity and skill with a gun, was just a kid.

And that kid was already at the street. Without glancing either way, he bolted across to the gate in the picket fence.

Fargo didn't make the same mistake. He halted before venturing into plain view. And it was then that a tall shape ambled from under the overhang to the front porch, a rifle in the crook of an elbow.

"Hold on there, boy. Where in tarnation do you reckon you're going?"

Wes had to be surprised but he hid it well. "I'm here to see my cousin, Susie. I won't take long. I promise."

"At this time of night?" The gunman was rightfully skeptical. "You're too young to be up this late. Do your folks know you're gallivanting around?"

"Who do you think sent me?" Wes blithely lied. "My cousin is feeling poorly and my mam has a stomach remedy that works wonders."

"Sick or not, Ira spread word that everybody is to stay indoors until morning. No one is excused. That includes you."

"Would you give it to her, then?" Moving toward the porch, Wes folded his arms in front of his waist so the man couldn't see the derringer. "My ma and pa sure would be obliged."

"What's their names? I must know them."

"Mosely," Wes said.

"Hell, boy. You being cute with me? Half the people in town are Moselys. I'm one my self. Horace Mosely. What are their first names? In which shack do they live?"

Wes was halfway there. "Mister, my cousin is awful sick. Can't you take the remedy to her and then I'll gladly tell you all about my folks?"

The man gazed at Lily's. "I'd like to, boy. But I could get in a heap of trouble. Ira said that whoever stands guard here isn't supposed to go in. I reckon he doesn't want us trifling with the fillies." He added sourly, "Not that Lily would let us if we could. Unless you've got coins to jingle, she doesn't let you set foot in the door."

"Please, mister." Wes only had a couple of yards to cover. "She's in terrible pain. Groaning and rolling around and such. Please take the medicine."

"Oh, all right. But if I get into hot water, you're going to be the one to tell Ira why I did it." Horace reached out. "Where's this remedy that's so damned important?"

"Right here," Wes said, and swept out the derringer. Ramming it into the guard's stomach, he fired once, twice, three times.

Fargo had anticipated as much and was racing across the street. The retorts were smothered by Horace's body, mere pops that shouldn't arouse much alarm. Wes jumped back and prepared to shoot again but the guard was crumpling, hands over his belly, astonishment washing over his face. Groaning, he twitched a few times, then went limp.

Wes spun as Fargo sped up the path. "Oh. It's just you."

"You should have waited for me," was all Fargo said. Kneeling, he examined Horace, who was still alive but breathing shallow. "Stay put, Wesley. And this time I mean it." Shoving the rifle at Wes to hold, Fargo dragged Mosely around the corner to the shrubs and concealed the unconscious form under them.

For once Wes listened. As casually as you please, he began to reload. "Not very bright, these Moselys and Henders," he commented.

"Bright enough to own a whole town," Fargo retorted briskly. "You were lucky. Most men wouldn't suspect anyone your age of being much of a threat."

"Their mistake." Wes closed the derringer. "Now what say we get this over with?" Bounding up the steps, he was at the door before Fargo could stop him.

"Wait. How are you going to find her? We can't go from door to door. It would make too much noise."

Wes lifted the latch. "I'll know her scent when I smell it. That stuff she splashes all over herself will draw me right to her."

"Her perfume?" Fargo said, thinking the very idea was preposterous. The boy had no idea of what a bawdy house was like. Every woman there was as fragrant as spring flowers. They sprinkled perfume in their bathwater, dabbed perfume on their ears, rubbed perfume on their necks, their shoulders, their breasts. Trying to isolate one scent out of the many was like looking for the proverbial needle in a haystack. "It can't be done. You're not a bloodhound."

"I know her smell real well," Wes said cryptically, and stole inside.

Wondering again how it was that a minister's son could be so ornery, Fargo trailed him in. The youngster tiptoed from door to door, sniffing at each. It was plain ridiculous, but Fargo had nothing better to suggest so he let Wes make a fool of himself. Most of the rooms were quiet, the women asleep. But from a few fluttered soft noises—rustling, cooing and the like. From one room on the second floor they heard loud groans, then a woman saying, "Yes! Yes! Harder! Harder!"

Wes glanced up. "What do you reckon they're doing?"

Fargo wouldn't say. Wes was much too young. Let him learn from his pa, or from experience. The latter was always the best teacher.

They moved to the next door. Once again Wes sniffed around the cracks and squatted to sniff close to the floor. Bounding up suddenly, he reached for the latch.

Fargo snatched his arm. "You can't go busting in there. What if it's not her?"

"It is, I tell you," Wes assured him. "Just let me take a peek. I won't give us away. I promise."

Against his better judgment, Fargo nodded. Wes opened the door slowly, an inch or so, and looked in. Going rigid, he showed more teeth than a politician on the stump, and leaped inside, pushing on the door so violently that Fargo had to catch it to keep it from slamming loud enough to wake everyone in Lily's. On a small table glowed a low lamp, casting just enough light to illuminate a bed against the left wall.

On it lay a young woman of nineteen or twenty. Blond curls framed her angelic features. She wore a plain cotton petticoat that had hiked above her knees, exposing nicely curved legs. Her lips, full as ripe berries, held the form of a perpetual pout. She was a true beauty, the kind of woman who turned heads on crowded thoroughfares.

Fargo closed the door and pressed an ear to the panel. No

commotion had resulted from the boy's blunder. They were safe enough, temporarily.

Wes, oddly, had halted, and was gaping at the blonde as if he had never seen her before. Taking tentative steps, he leaned on the bed and tenderly stroked her luxuriant hair, then jerked his hand back as if he'd touched broken glass. "Susie?" he whispered.

The woman was sound asleep.

"Susie?" Wes repeated, shaking her lightly.

She stirred, rolling from her side onto her back, her bosom rising like twin mountains, straining against her petticoat. In profile she was exquisitely gorgeous.

Impatient, Wes shook her harder.

The young woman smacked her lips as if eating tasty food, then mumbled and opened her eyes. She blinked up at Wes, puzzled, then recognizing him, came up off the bed beaming. "Wesley! Is that you?" Clapping him on the shoulders, she swung her feet to the floor and held him at arm's length to examine him. "How in the world? What are you doing here? Where did—" She caught sight of Fargo, and stopped. "Hold it. Who's he? What's going on?"

Wes placed a hand on her arm. "Susie? Is it really you? I almost didn't know who you were. What have they done to your hair? And what's all that stuff on your cheeks and your mouth? And these clothes?"

Susan Dixon smoothed her petticoat and sat the boy down beside her. "Listen," she said quietly, "I don't know why you're here, but you have to go."

"Why else?" Wes declared loudly. "I came to save you. To fetch you home, where you belong."

"Hush," Susan said. "Keep your voice down or we'll have Lily in here, and she'll throw you out on your ear." Smiling, she removed his hat and ruffled his hair. "Wessy, I just can't believe it. Do you mean to tell me that you came all this way on my account? Oh, that's so sweet. No one looks after me like you do."

Fargo had never seen the boy blush but Wes did so now, growing as red as a beet.

"Who brought you, Wessy?" Susan asked. "Is Rafe along? Or maybe Joel? Are they waiting outside?"

"No, just me."

"You came *alone*?"

In pure adoration Wes gazed into her bright blue eyes. "When I heard what your pa had done, I almost shot him. I went over to your place and found him on the floor, drunk. His derringers were in the drawer where they always are, so I loaded them and put one to his head but I couldn't pull the trigger. I was afraid it would upset you."

"Oh, Wessy, you didn't."

"Yep. I sure did. Then I lit out after you but I rode my pony to death. It's been one problem after another ever since."

Susan studied Fargo. "What about you, mister? Where do you fit in? I don't recollect ever seeing you in Sumpter or at any of the socials."

Wes answered. "He's not from home. He's a friend of mine I picked up along the way. Forget about him. I want to know about you." Wes raised a hand to her golden curls. "What have they done to you, Susie? Look at your hair. It used to be so fine and straight. Now you're all made up like some of those ladies we used to see over to Galveston. Only prettier, of course."

Susie Dixon kissed him on the forehead. Fargo thought Wes had blushed red before, but that wasn't anything compared to the scarlet flush that crept over him now.

"I did all this to myself, Wessy," Susan said. "Oh, some of the ladies here helped. But I like doing up my hair and such. Pa never let me. I always had to go around looking like a wet mop."

"It'll take some getting used to," Wes said. "The important thing is, I found you and you're safe. Now let's light a shuck. In a week you'll be home where you belong. Everything will be just like it was."

Susan shifted, pursing her sensational lips. She looked at Fargo, and he guessed what was coming. "It's not that simple, I'm afraid."

"Why not?"

"I can't go back, Wessy."

The boy clutched her. "I understand. They're holding you against your will. But they won't stop us. I won't let them. I'll shoot anyone who gets in our way."

Growing sad, Susan Dixon slid closer to him and draped an arm across his shoulders. "No, it's not anything like that. The plain truth is, I don't want to go. Sure, my pa sold me to these people. But it's only for a year. And I like it here, Wessy. I truly do. They treat me real nice. I have new clothes and shoes. Jewelry, too, the first I've ever owned." She ran a fingertip over a necklace she had on. "It beats waiting on Pa hand and foot. It beats slopping hogs and plowing fields and doing housework from dawn till dusk."

Wes's Adam's apple bounced up and down. "But, Susie. These people are bad. I've seen what they do to girls like you. They'll kill you if you ever cross them."

"Why would I want to cross them?" Susan responded. "You're talking nonsense. They've treated me like a princess since I arrived. Lily is testy sometimes, but only when we don't abide by her rules."

Wes appealed to Fargo. "Tell her. Tell her about Sline and how things are. Tell her about Ira."

Susan brightened. "You've met them? I haven't been introduced to Mr. Hender yet, but Mr. Sline has been a perfect gentleman. Where did you run into him? Here in town?"

"No, up at his cabin," Wes said. "We just killed him."

"You did what? You can't be serious. Why would you harm a sweet man like him? He brought me here, Wessy. He set me up in this fine house with these fine ladies. Please say it's not so."

Fargo couldn't blame the boy for what he did next. Which was to jump to his feet and violently shake Susan, as if by doing so he'd shake some sense into her.

"Listen to me, Susie! Please! Sline was a polecat, through and through! Ira Hender is no better! They use pretty gals like you. And when they're done with you, they'll murder you and toss you out on the prairie for the scavengers to eat."

"Keep your voice down!" Susan said.

But the harm had been done. From various points in the house pealed questioning voices. Down the hall a door opened. Fargo put his shoulder to the panel, whispering to the blonde, "He's right. You've been hoodwinked by a bunch of badmen who will snuff you out like a candle once you're no longer of any use to them."

"Who *are* you? A lawman?"

A commotion in the hall signaled they were short of time. "We have to leave, now," Fargo said. "We'll go out the back door and circle to our horses."

"Like hell!" Susan stood, fists on her hips. "I'm not going anywhere! Haven't you heard a word I've said? I like it here! I truly and really do! I get all the nice things I've ever wanted, and all I have to do is cuddle with a few men every day."

"Susie!" Wes exclaimed.

"What's wrong with that?" the blonde said defensively. "Men have been pawing me ever since I can remember. Most of the time I'd slap them silly. Well, now they get to, but they pay Lily for the privilege and she passes on some of the money to me. I like the arrangement."

"But it's wrong. Ladies shouldn't do it. Pa says—"

Susan cut him off. "What does your stuffy old pa know? He's not the only one who's read some of the Bible. I know for a fact there are women in there who sell their bodies for money. So don't act so high and mighty, John Wesley—"

Pounding on the door drowned out the rest of what she said. Fargo held the latch so it couldn't be moved and felt someone try. There were no locks, a precaution in case customers became too rowdy and the women needed rescuing. From the sound of things, everyone in the bawdy house was rushing to Dixon's room. "We have to get out, now!" Fargo commanded.

Wes grabbed his cousin and tugged but she wouldn't budge. "Please, Susie! You heard him. We have to skedaddle."

"Don't either of you have ears?" his cousin snapped. "This is the best deal I've ever had. I'm not going back, not to Pa and that wretched farm and hard work day after day after day. I refuse!"

In the hallway, Lily Hender called out. "Susan? Susan, dear? What's happening in there? Who's in there with you?"

"It's my cousin!" Susan replied.

"Your who? Why can't we open the door? Open it this instant or we'll have to kick it in."

There wasn't a moment to lose. Fargo jumped back, angled the Henry at the door, and sent two slugs crashing through it. He aimed high enough not to hit anyone on the other side. But they didn't know that. Screeching and swearing, they scrambled to make themselves scarce before he fired again, which he had no intention of doing.

Whirling toward the window, Fargo flung it open. The room was on the same side of the house as the shrubs, which were directly below. "This will do," he said. "Wes, you go first."

"I'm not leaving without Susie."

In the hall, Lily was yelling for everyone to quiet down. In the street, a few shouts let Fargo know that Caleb or Hiram had heard the shots and would be investigating soon. "We need to leave now, or we'll never make it," he said.

Wes was a living portrait of confusion and dismay. "I'm begging you, Susie! Come with us. I'll explain everything later."

A heavy blow shook the door. Then another. "Put your shoulder into it, Arlan!" Lily commanded. "As big as you are, you'll knock it off its hinges."

Again the door trembled from the tremendous impact. Wes stared at it, his face undergoing a startling change, a transformation from childish confusion to a mask of utter fury. "Leave us be!" he hollered, drawing the derringer in a blur. More rapidly than most grown men could do, he sent two shots into the door. But where Fargo had aimed high, Wes aimed squarely at the center. Someone bellowed like a gored bull elk, and some women screamed. "Leave us be!" Wes railed again, triggering another shot, a little lower this time.

"They've killed him! They've murdered Arlan!" a woman bawled.

Everything had gone to hell. Fargo raised the window higher and leaned the Henry against the wall. Soon the whole town would be in an uproar. Getting away would be out of the question. Darting to Susan Dixon, he looped an arm around her waist.

"Let go of me! I don't want to go, damn you!"

Lady Luck was on her side. For when Fargo swept her to the window, he saw two men sprint into sight below. Their only avenue of escape had been cut off!

# 9

With each passing moment, the likelihood that Skye Fargo would leave Hender's Gap with his hide intact grew less and less. The two men outside had drawn their revolvers and were scanning the windows. They weren't sure which room the shots had come from. More blows resounded against the door. The people in the hallway didn't realize they could work the latch if they tried, and they were still attempting to batter the door in. And while all this was going on, Susan Dixon struggled fiercely to be free of Fargo's grasp. The young woman had no inkling of what lay in store for her. To her, Hender's Gap was heaven, and in her ignorance she was helping to foil the only chance she had of being saved.

All these elements Fargo had to consider, then act on. "Wes!" he shouted above the uproar, and the boy promptly dashed to his side. "Put another slug through the door."

Without hesitation, the youngster did so, momentarily stopping the barrage of blows. Lusty curses were flung at them.

At the derringer's bang, the two men outside looked up at their window. "Quick! Shoot at them," Fargo directed, even though the pair were out of the derringer's effective range. Wes complied, and while he didn't hit either one, the men sought cover, running back around the corner.

Susan had briefly stopped struggling, but now she resumed, kicking and hitting and caterwauling, "Let go of me! Let go, damn it!"

"Whatever you say," Fargo replied. Swinging her out the window, he released her.

It was difficult to say who was more shocked, Susan or Wes. She screamed, and he almost leaped out the window after her. Wes tried to snag her ankles but missed, his cry of despair following her down. Both had forgotten about the thick shrubs.

Susan crashed onto them. The plants cushioned her fall as well as a mattress would do, the jolt of striking the ground not much worse than it would have been had she fallen from a first-floor window. She was scraped and nicked, but that was all.

The two gunmen saw her plummet and ran toward her. Fargo, pushing Wes aside, scooped up the Henry and brought it to bear just as one of the gunmen fired at him. Lead bit into the sill, slivers of wood flying every which way. His answering shot slammed into the man's right leg. The second gunman jumped to help his friend, supporting him as they retreated again, both shooting wildly.

Wes kept trying to poke his head out the window to see his cousin. "How is she?" he asked over and over.

"Find out for yourself." So saying, Fargo put down the rifle, seized the boy by the shoulders, and propelled him out the window. To his credit, Wes didn't cry out, and twisted on the way down so he landed feet-first.

Fargo was right behind him. Clutching the Henry, he smashed through the shrubbery onto his hands and knees, then spun toward the street. Lamps had been lit in one of the buildings, and a knot of men were rushing from the hotel.

"Susie! Are you all right?" Wes was at her side, helping her stand, but she wanted nothing to do with him and slapped his arm away.

"Leave me alone!"

Fargo saw a gunman pop out from the corner. His Henry blasted, catapulting the man rearward. He yelled to the boy,

"Run! Get to the horses!" Heeding his own advice, he broke for the picket fence. Behind him a pistol cracked. Pivoting, he fixed a bead on a silhouette in the window and hammered off two shots. Then he was in motion again, lead sizzling the air from several directions. Reaching the fence, he paused to insure Wes was at his heels, but the boy and the blonde hadn't moved. They still bickered, Wes attempting to spur her on and Susan refusing.

"Wes! Forget about her!" Fargo urged, but he might as well have urged the wind to stop blowing. It was obvious the boy wouldn't desert her, even at the cost of his own life.

That put Fargo in a quandary. Another armed figure had materialized in the window, more gunmen were coming around the front of the house, and the street was swiftly filling with people and flying lead. He had to get them out of there *now* or he never would.

Fargo could still escape on his own. A bound would take him over the fence. He would be in among the shacks on the other side of the street before anyone could stop him, but that would mean leaving the boy behind.

"Son of a bitch," Fargo said to no one in particular as he brought up the Henry. The tubular magazine under the barrel held fifteen shells, and to the best of his recollection he had used six. That left nine. He fired at the figure in the window. He dropped two hard cases speeding from out front. He sprayed three shots at the street, felling a couple more. His intent was to draw attention away from the boy and the woman, and in that he succeeded admirably.

A ragged volley forced Fargo to drop below the fence. He shifted as a burly shape dove past the corner, fanning a revolver, an unreliable tactic at best. Fargo's own shot taught a terminal lesson that left the man flopping in the dirt like a buckshot goose.

Footsteps thudded. Wes had finally come to his senses. Tears dampening his cheeks, he pitched onto his knees and said forlornly, "She just won't go."

"Forget her! The important thing is for us to get out

alive!" Fargo palmed the Colt. "Can you hold them back while I reload?"

A savage glint lit the boy's eyes. "Just see if I don't." Wedging the derringer under his belt, he held the heavy Colt in both hands and heaved to his feet. The men in the street and those at the front were boldly surging forward, and Wes winged lead at both groups, the big Colt bucking in his small hands. Those in front scurried to safety while those in the street flattened.

Eight or nine guns boomed at once. A swarm of slugs would have riddled Wes had Fargo not grabbed him and pulled him low. "After you fire, get down!"

"Sorry," the youngster said. Incredibly, he showed no fear, not a lick of it. Curling back the hammer, he waited while the firing tapered off, then sprang up and zinged a slug at a rifleman in a lower floor window.

Fargo was reloading as furiously as he was able. Six, seven, eight rounds he replaced, when suddenly the townsmen made a concerted attack from all quarters. Seizing Wes by the back of the shirt, he hurled the boy over the fence, then vaulted after him. Bullets thumped into the rail, punching holes, shattering wood.

"That way!" Fargo hollered, giving Wes a shove toward the shacks. "I'll cover you!" To that end, he unfurled and fired at the crowd so they would keep hugging the ground. Those at the front of the house were spreading out across the yard, their pistols and rifles flaring like fireflies. Rotating, Fargo drilled the one most eager to die. Wes shot, too, and together they gained the shacks and safety.

"We did it!" the boy declared.

Hardly. The horses were still hundreds of yards away. Fargo took several loping strides, then halted abruptly when a heavy-set form appeared ahead.

It was Caleb Hender, his tin star glinting dully, his thumbs hooked in his gunbelt. He made no move for his six-shooters. Grinning, he bellowed in the momentary lull of the din, "No more shooting, boys! You hear me! No one is to fire!"

A few seconds of silence ensued, and then someone shouted, "Caleb, is that you?"

"No, it's Abraham Lincoln!" the lawman rejoined. "Of course it's me, you jackass! Do as I say! I've caught them!"

"You have?" Fargo said, elevating the Henry. But he didn't fire. Caleb was much too confident, like a five-card stud player with an ace in the hole.

Wes extended the Colt. "Let me! I've never killed a law-dog!"

Caleb, chuckling, lifted his arms out from his sides. "Go right ahead, brat. Buck me out in gore. You, too, mister. But know this. If I die, your redheaded friend dies, as well."

"Elsie?" Fargo had feared as much. It was the final straw. Everything that could go wrong had gone wrong. She'd gone and gotten herself caught, and now the three of them were maggot fodder.

"How do we know this tub of bear fat isn't bluffing?" Wes asked. "Let's give him a new nose." He sighted along the revolver.

"Bloodthirsty little turd, aren't you?" Caleb said.

Fargo placed a hand on the Colt and tilted the barrel at the ground. "No. It's not a bluff. Elsie's death would be on your head. Do you want that?"

"I reckon not," Wes said, taking his finger off the trigger. "Even if she is addlepated, she's a lady. And ladies shouldn't ever be hurt."

Caleb snickered and advanced. "Boy, you have a lot to learn. There's no such thing as a lady. Women are no better than we are. They like to put on fancy airs, but they sweat and spit and break wind like we do."

"My pa told me about men like you," Wes said in disgust. "Men who can't see past their own chamber pots."

Snorting, Caleb replied, "What the hell does that have to do with anything? Your pa must be one of those yacks who puts all women on thrones and worships them."

"Say one bad thing about my father," Wes said, "and I'll

turn you from a bull into a steer. No one insults my kin." He tried to elevate the Colt but Fargo wouldn't let him.

Caleb stopped and scratched his chin. "I believe you would, sprout. It's too bad you're not a Hender. You have the makings of a real man." His pudgy hands reached out. "Your guns, if you please."

Moving shadows flitted on all sides, weapons bristling like quills on a porcupine. To resist was pointless. Fargo and Wes were roughly seized and marched toward the Hender Hotel at the center of an angry mob.

"They killed Sloane and Dirk and Tom!" a bearded ruffian grumbled.

"We should string them up and be done with it!" said someone else.

"Hell, a necktie social is too good for 'em. We should stake 'em out under the broiling sun!"

"Why not skin them alive and hang them from a tree by their ankles? They'd take days to die!"

Caleb nipped the debate in the bud by informing them, "Ira wants these jaspers alive. He'll decide what to do once he's questioned them. Any complaints, take it up with him."

Four guards flanked the ramp. The door was open, and just inside were Hiram and the beanpole. Other bodyguards surrounded the platform on which reposed the repulsive lord of the Hender clan. Many more were present. Sam, Charley, and ten or eleven others were also in attendance. In a group by themselves was a motley assortment of hard cases, the outlaws who had paid for the right to hide out in Hender's Gap. Some women huddled against the right wall.

But it was the person beside Ira who interested Fargo most. Elsie was on her knees, her wrists bound behind her back. A rope had been looped around her neck, the rest coiled close to the divan. Her eyes gazed vacantly off into nowhere, as if she were dead inside. Blood dappled her chin.

Caleb proudly strode to the divan. After the last of the mob had filed into the chamber, he sneered at his captives and said, "Here they are, Pa. The two troublemakers. It was just like you said. They didn't lift a finger once they knew we had the woman."

Up close, Ira Hender was more hideous than Fargo had imagined. His immense bulk, moon-eyes, and huge teeth conspired to give Fargo the impression he stood before something unhuman. It was unsettling. Fargo smiled at Elsie but she was adrift in her own inner world.

"So, I meet the famed Trailsman in person," Ira rumbled. "Strange. To me, you're as puny as everyone else." He sat up. "Tell me, Skye Fargo. What brings a man with your reputation to my humble town?"

Fargo recalled the conversation he'd overheard between father and son. "The government sent me," he lied.

It had an effect. Ira's great ogre face creased in deep thought as his sausage arms pumped his enormous hulk erect. "Is that a fact? I'd considered as much."

Caleb lacked his father's intellect, which, ironically, made him less gullible. "He's lyin', Pa. Did the government send the brat, too? No, he's here with the boy to save the boy's cousin. That's all there is to it. And she'll be here any minute to prove I'm right."

Wes had been as tame as a kitten since being caught, but at the mention of Susan he lunged at the lawman. "Hurt her, fat man, and you die!" The gunman holding him jerked him back.

"Behave, kid."

Ira waddled from his perch, down a short ramp, and over to Fargo, looming like a living mountain. Warm, rank breath fanned Fargo's face as the patriarch bent to study him. "Is my son right for once? Are you tellin' the truth? Or being clever in the vain hope it will spare your life?"

Fargo hadn't played poker for years for nothing. "Reports have come in to the rangers and federal marshals. Reports about missing women. With the Comanches acting up, and word of a break between the South and the North, they're busy elsewhere. So a ranger friend asked me to sniff around."

Ira lifted a hand toward Wes, who pulled back as if it were a scorpion. "And this lad? Where does he fit into the scheme of things?"

"I met him on my way here," Fargo said. "His cousin is one of the women who went missing. So I decided to help him out."

"Kill two birds with one stone?" Ira said. "I see. Your story is plausible. But if there's one lesson life has taught me, it's never take anyone at their word. Not even my own flesh and blood."

At that moment two of the hard cases walked up. One was a scruffy wolf who hadn't bathed in a year. The other had on a black frock coat and a broad-brimmed black hat, the earmarks of a professional gambler.

Ira addressed them without looking around. "What can I do for you gentlemen?"

"We had us a parley," said the scruffy onion. "Vin and me were picked to do the talking for everyone else."

"Is that so, Fritz?" Ira had to pivot his entire body to face them. His thick neck wouldn't turn far enough. "I take it you have a grievance to air? If so, you would do well to remember what happened to the last man who presumed on my good nature."

Fritz gulped and clammed up, but the gambler wasn't cowed. "Threats don't sit well with me, Hender. So I'd be civil, unless you want every last one of us to saddle up and leave."

"What about the money you've paid for sanctuary, Vincent? I've made it plain I don't give refunds."

"You can keep your damn money, for all we care," the gambler said. "But how much more do you think you'll earn after we spread word that the deal you offer isn't as foolproof as you make it out to be?"

In light of One-Eared John's fate, Fargo marveled that anyone had the nerve to stand up to Ira. He noticed the gambler's hands were held closer to the ends of his sleeves, hinting that Wes wasn't the only person fond of derringers.

"I wouldn't earn much," the town's founder conceded. "So instead of slingin' verbal stones, why don't we reason together like rational men should?"

The gambler's courage was contagious. Fritz thrust his chest out and said, "You're partial to slinging big words, ain't you? But they don't amount to much."

"Are you callin' me a liar?" Ira responded with such venom his bodyguards fingered their rifles.

Vin frowned at Fritz, then said, "It's not that, Hender. We trust you. We know you're a man of your word. But life is like a game of cards. No matter how well we stack the deck, sometimes we're dealt cards we didn't expect."

"Well phrased," Ira said.

"You promised us we'd be safe here, that we could hide out right under the law's nose, and so far things have gone exactly as you predicted." Vin looked at Fargo. "But now he shows up. A wild card. And all hell breaks loose."

"Aren't you makin' a mountain out of an ant hill?"

"Am I? Five or six of your clan are dead, we hear. Sline's place has been burned to the ground with him in it. One-Eared John is dead."

"It's a coincidence our late friend died about the same time Fargo arrived. As for the rest, you can see I have the situation completely under control."

Vin held his ground. "Sorry, Ira. We see no such thing. And all this talk about the marshals and the Texas Rangers doesn't help. For all we know, a company of soldiers is on its way here right this minute. We'd rather not be here when they show up."

The fleshy seams of Ira's face quivered with suppressed anger. "What are you saying, Vincent? You're going to carry out your threat?"

"No. We're going up in the hills for a few days and lie low. When we come back, we hope to find everything just as it was. If the rangers or the marshals haven't paid you a visit, if Fargo has been taken care of, if there are no more problems, we'll stay. But if there's any more trouble—" The gambler left the statement unfinished.

"I see," Ira rumbled. Clearly, he did not like it, not one bit. His huge toadlike eyes roved over the outlaws, boring into each and every one. A few nervously shifted and averted their faces. His scowl became a crevice.

"It's nothing personal," the gambler added to soothe him. "Hell, we know you've taken every precaution possible. And we know how much our business arrangement means to you."

"Do you, Vincent? I think not." Ira motioned. "Look around you. All the people, all the buildings, depend on the money we earn from men like you who need a safe haven. It's our life's blood, if you will. Our whole economy is based on it. Without the income, in a year or two Hender's Gap would be a ghost town." The ogre's moon face grew as hard as quartz. "I refuse to let that happen. My kin depend on me. They trust me. After the law became too interested in our activities back home they came all this way to start over, just on my say-so."

"You have your family to think of, we have our safety," Vin said. "Don't let us down, and before you know it, things will be back to normal."

"Oh, have no fear in that regard."

Fingers as thick as cucumbers clamped onto Fargo's shoulder and squeezed. Agony knifed through him, and he nearly fell to his knees. He was astonished by Hender's strength. It was as immense as the man's size.

"When you and the others return, Vincent, all the loose ends will have been tied up. Our famous interloper has come to the end of his trail. We'll put out the word he was killed in a saloon brawl, shot in the back by a drunk after they argued over a game of cards." Ira removed his hand. "Word is, he's quite fond of gamblin'. So it shouldn't make his friends in high places suspicious."

The gambler headed for the door and the other hard cases tromped after him. "Whatever you do is fine by us, Ira. Just so it's all settled when we get back." At the entrance, he stopped. "You have three days. And remember, Fargo isn't the only one with a lot of friends." The badmen filed out.

For a minute no one spoke. All eyes were on the patriarch, who stood as if chiseled from stone. At last Ira made a sound, a snarl such as a gigantic bear might make, and said, "Did you hear him, Caleb? Did you hear him threaten me? *Me?*"

"I heard, Pa, Those vermin need to be taught who's boss here. Want me to round some of the boys and stop them from leavin'?"

"No. I want you to think, son. Use your brain. One day I'll be gone and you'll be the new head of the clan. As such, you have to put the welfare of your kin above all else." Ira lumbered toward the divan. "If you tried to make them stay, they would resent it. They might resort to gunplay. Kill just one of them without due cause, and there won't be an outlaw in the whole state of Texas who will be willin' to pay us for sanctuary."

"So we let them tell us what we should and shouldn't do?"

"Sometimes a man has to swallow his pride in order to keep it." Ira started up the ramp, moving stiffly. "I swear. If my knees get any worse, I'll have to roll wherever I want to go." Sighing loudly, he sank onto the divan and picked up the end of the rope looped around Elsie's neck. "Now let's tend to business."

As if on cue, a commotion at the far doorway heralded the arrival of six members of the clan, pushing two women ahead of them. One was Susan Dixon. The other, to Fargo's surprise, was Madelyn Mosely. Susan was scared half to death and jumped each time she was shoved. Madelyn shoved back, cursing them. But she ceased as they neared the platform, focusing her ire on their leader.

"What the hell is going on, Ira? Why was I dragged here against my will? Since when do you treat a cousin like an outsider?"

Ira rested his cucumber fingers in his lap. "My dear Maddy. Such indignation ill becomes you. Haven't you always been near and dear to me? Haven't I favored you over all other Moselys by lettin' you run the saloon? You have a great head for business. As well as other great assets."

Caleb and some of the guards smirked.

"You are here, Madelyn," Ira went on, "because it has come to my attention that my trust in you might be misplaced. That maybe you aren't as loyal to your kin as you should be."

The brunette glanced at Fargo, whose eyes told her to watch what she said around this evil ogre of a man. "I've always been devoted to you, Ira. I've never lied, never cheated you. You yourself said I was completely reliable."

"That was back when you were," Ira said. "But now you've given me cause to doubt you. To question whether you put the welfare of your flesh and blood above all else, as you should."

Madelyn fearlessly walked up to the platform. "Quit bandyin' words. What could I have possibly done?"

Ira gave it to her with both barrels. "You screwed Mr. Fargo."

Fargo saw her flinch as if she had been struck. But she was quick to regain her composure, her chin jutting defiantly.

"Who says I did?"

"Please, don't insult my intelligence. I have my ways of learnin' things."

Madelyn tried another approach. "Isn't that what you expect of us girls at the saloon? To entice customers over to Lily's for a frolic under the sheets? I didn't do anything with him that I haven't done with more men than I can shake a stick at."

Ira's great belly shook with silent mirth. "I've always admired your cleverness, but now you've tripped over it. Yes, the women at the saloon drum up business for my daughter. But you, my dear, have drummed up less then anyone else.

You'd much rather be behind the bar than in bed. I've tolerated your reluctance because you have such a good head for business." He paused. "For you to sleep with Mr. Fargo is unusual. For you to do so and not report it to me is a serious breach."

"I'm supposed to let you know when I make love?" Madelyn said sarcastically.

"Ordinarily, no. But you knew I was huntin' for him. Caleb told you. You knew the whole town was being combed, that everyone was under orders to report his whereabouts. Yet, much to my dismay, you didn't. You let Fargo come and go as he pleased, and now many of our kin are dead due to your neglect."

Madelyn's feistiness was fading fast. "He threatened to kill me if I said anything."

"That won't hold up in the wash, Maddy," Ira rebutted. "You could have gone to Lily or Caleb after Fargo left. Why didn't you? I'll tell you. Because you've turned traitor."

Susan Dixon had been wringing her hands in an excess of anxiety. Suddenly she bawled, "What about me, Mr. Hender? I'm no traitor, I like it here."

Ira showed his huge teeth. "More's the pity, child. You see, since the boy came after you, it gives me cause to think others might. And the last thing I need right now is undue interest in my affairs. So I'm afraid I have no recourse."

"No!" Susan mewed.

"Yes." Ira glared at all four of them in turn. "You're all going to die."

# 10

Susan Dixon blubbered from the moment they left Hender's Gap until they reached their destination. Her endless crying, loud sniffling, and pitiable whining irritated Caleb so much that at one point he wheeled his sorrel and slapped her.

"Quit your bawlin', gal! Or I'll slit that pretty throat of yours and dump you for the buzzards to eat!"

"But I haven't *done* anything!" The blonde sobbed. "You can't blame me for what my cousin did! He's just a boy! He doesn't know any better!"

Skye Fargo happened to be staring at Wes and saw the hurt she'd inflicted. The youngster had gone through literal hell to save her, and she repaid him with insults. Behind the boy rode Madelyn, her wrists tied behind her back like the rest of them. She held herself straight in the saddle, refusing to give the nine men Ira had picked to conduct them to their deaths the satisfaction of seeing her grovel.

Fargo pretended to be depressed over his impending fate and rode with his shoulders slumped. But he had every hope of turning the tables. For in all the excitement when he was captured, no one had thought to frisk him. The Arkansas toothpick rested securely in its ankle sheath. All they had to do was leave him alone for a minute and he could cut himself free. The big question was whether they would.

To still be alive was a minor miracle in itself. Fargo had figured Ira would have them taken out and shot, but no, the devil had different plans. He'd ordered them to be taken to "the gulch," the name of which caused chortling among the men, as if at some secret jest.

Now they were miles from town, high in the hills to the southwest. The burning sun baked them dry. A hot breeze offered no relief as a winding narrow trail took them deeper and deeper into Nature's oven. It was only the middle of the morning, yet the only living thing abroad was a lizard.

Fargo had been rubbing his wrists together for so long, they were rubbed raw. He glanced at Elsie, who hadn't uttered a peep all night. Whatever Ira Hender had done to her had totally broken her spirit. Hender finished what Jacob Sline had started, and now the redhead was an empty shell, a mindless doll who didn't know where she was or what she was doing.

In order to learn more about what was in store for them, Fargo asked Caleb, "How much further to the gulch? And what's so special about it?"

"You'll find out soon enough, mister," was the lawman's response. "I wouldn't complain about how long it takes to get there. The sooner we do, the sooner you'll fry in hell."

Susan blubbered anew, pleading, "Don't do this to me, Caleb. I've always treated you nice, haven't I? Spare me, and I'll be yours and yours alone from here on out. Your father won't need to know."

"You want me to buck Pa?" It struck Caleb as hilarious. "Girl, that'd be the same as puttin' a loaded gun to my head and pullin' the trigger. My being his flesh and blood won't count for a hill of beans."

"But don't you fancy me?" Susan asked, arching her back so her nipples were outlined against the chemise. "You did the other night. You said I was the sweetest sugar you've ever tasted."

"You could be made of molasses, for all the good it would do you," Caleb said. "No female is worth an early grave. Just be thankful Pa didn't have your neck stretched. Or do to you like he did to the redhead."

They were climbing toward a sawtooth spine, and one of the gunmen declared, "We're almost there!"

"Thank God," Caleb said. "A man can only take so much snivelin'."

The barren crest overlooked a narrow gulch with steep slopes littered by rocks of all shapes and sizes. A horse would never make it to the bottom in one piece. Which was why the trail ended at the brink. Fargo, the three women, and Wes were hauled from their mounts and prodded to the rim. Sixty feet below were sharp, jagged boulders.

Fargo tensed, thinking they were to be pushed to a gory end, but instead the men stepped back, some leveling rifles. So they were to be shot, after all, Fargo thought, and coiled his leg muscles to pounce. To give up without a struggle wasn't in his nature. He'd resist until his dying breath.

Caleb was last to climb down. "What are you simpletons standin' around for?" he remarked. "Over the edge you go."

"You want us to jump?" Madelyn asked.

"Honey, I don't care if you jump, fly, or wriggle. Just start down. We won't shoot you in the back, if that's what's worryin' you. I give you my word."

Fargo stared at the bottom again. With a little luck they could make it all the way down, and once they did, the boulders would protect them from gunfire. But Caleb would never allow that. There had to be a hitch, something he wasn't aware of.

"What are you waitin' for?" the lawman demanded. "Winter? Go, or we'll give each of you a push."

None of the women moved, and Fargo couldn't blame them. Wes took a step but Fargo quickly moved past him so he was the first on the slope. The ground was firm, not talus, as he'd feared. The rocks were large enough for him to hop from one to the other, like stepping stones across a stream. Although the incline was steep, it wasn't steep enough to cause them to lose their footing unless they were careless. He foresaw no problem in descending.

The gulch ran east to west. Accordingly, it was in the sun

all day. It caught the first rays of dawn and the last shafts of twilight. On hot days like this, it was a boiling cauldron, and Fargo had to squint against the glare.

John Wesley, Fargo couldn't help noting, was a cauldron himself. Hatred oozed from the boy like wax from a candle. When any of the clan touched him, he jerked away or tried to kick them. His expression was that of a mad dog aglow with bloodlust. He was a keg of black powder waiting for the right spark to set him off.

Fargo was twenty feet below the rim when the boy lurched to a stop, one foot lifted as if he had been about to step on something he shouldn't. A distinct rattling filled the gulch, like small stones being jiggled in a sluice, only magnified, so it seemed to come from everywhere and anywhere at once.

"A rattler! Don't move!" Fargo said, slanting to help. Sinuous movement almost underfoot stopped him cold. At the same instant, he realized it wasn't an echo he was hearing—there were more snakes. Many more. The gulch was where they came to sun themselves, to breed, and probably to nest in during the winter. It was where they congregated by the scores, if not the hundreds. As his eyes adjusted to the glare, Fargo discovered more and more of them, curled up on, under, and around the rocks. The gulch literally crawled with serpents.

Mocking laughter from above was drowned out by Susan Dixon's scream. She was as pale as a sheet, agape at a snake slithering by.

"No one move!" Fargo directed. Wes had already frozen. Madelyn was on a wide, flat rock, terrified but biting on her lower lip to keep from imitating Susan. Elsie, however, was shambling lower, taking small, halting steps, oblivious to what was happening.

"Stop!" Madelyn yelled.

The redhead didn't heed. Susan was nearest to her, so Fargo pivoted and said, "Grab her before she's bit!" But the blonde was too petrified. He'd have to do it himself. Leaping from one large rock to another, each time provoking more hisses and rattles, Fargo reached Elsie and stopped her by putting his shoulder against her chest. It was the best he could do with his arms tied. "Be still," he whispered in her ear.

The men from town were cackling. Caleb stepped as close to the rock field as he dared and drew the Smith & Wessons. "You don't seem to understand. I want you to keep going, clear to the bottom."

"We'll never make it!" Susan screeched. "There are too many!"

Caleb snorted. "That's the whole point. The fun is to see how soon the snakes bring you down. Once we had an hombre who almost made it but he tripped. When he got back up, he had snakes hanging from his neck, his face, everywhere."

Madelyn twisted toward him. "I always knew you were a bastard, Caleb. But I never realized how big a bastard until right now."

"You're mighty sassy for someone who isn't going to live out the hour," Caleb bantered. Then he cocked the Smith & Wessons. "Since you're not enterin' into the spirit of things, I reckon I'll have to help you along."

"You promised you wouldn't shoot us!" Susan cried.

"And I'll keep my word, missy. I'll be shootin' at your feet to spur you along, is all. If I miss and nick you, well, don't hold it against me. It's hard to aim when I'm laughin' hard enough to bust a gut."

Madelyn was livid. "You're a pig, Caleb, just like your pa. I hope one day the Moselys stop playin' second fiddle to the Henders and rise up against the whole mangy passel of you."

Caleb grinned at the other men. "Isn't she something, boys? All these years, and she hasn't gotten it through her thick head. To us, our kin are everything. We live for them. We'd die for them. It doesn't matter whether we're a Hender or a Mosely. We're all equals." He looked at Madelyn.

"No wonder you turned on us, gal. Your blood is tainted. I bet your ma trifled with an outsider."

"She never!" Madelyn replied. "She was always loyal to the family!"

"Which is more than we can say about you." Caleb pointed the pistols. "Now then. Everyone ready? On the count of three."

"No!" Susan shrieked. "For the love of God!"

"In case you ain't noticed, dearie, the Almighty lets us fend for ourselves. When we die, we die. It doesn't matter how." Caleb paused. "One."

Madelyn stared down the slope, then at him. "Shoot me. I'd rather go quick than slow. A bullet is a lot less painful than venom in my veins."

"Sorry. The whole purpose is for you to suffer. A mercy killin' would spoil everything." Again Caleb paused for effect. "Two."

Fargo put his lips against Elsie's ear. It was hopeless but he had to try. "We have to run, Elsie. Do you hear me? We must make it to the bottom without getting bit." She didn't react, didn't move a muscle. "There are rattlesnakes all over. Most won't strike unless you step on them, or come close." Rattlers were notorious man-killers, but the truth was that nine times out of ten, they would rather flee than fight. It was the tenth time a person had to watch out for.

"Three!" Caleb said, and the Smith & Wessons thundered, one methodical shot after another, the slugs kicking up dust and sending chips flying.

Susan was his first target. She screamed as bullets nearly clipped her legs. Hopping like a rabbit, she lit out down the slope, bawling as she ran, her eyes so filled with tears she couldn't possibly see where she was going. And maybe that was for the best, Fargo reasoned, because the sight of all those snakes would have stopped her dead and given them a chance to strike.

Wes didn't wait to be goaded. He ran after his cousin,

staying close to her, acting as protector even when he could do little to help.

Caleb pivoted and fired at Madelyn's feet. For a few moments she glared at him. Then a piece of rock ripped her lower leg open, and she flinched and almost fell. Righting herself just in time, she began hopping from rock to rock as Fargo had done, avoiding those on which rattlesnakes were coiled.

Fargo said to Elsie, "Go! Run!" and nudged her with his shoulder. All she did was stumble, though, and resume plodding downward, paying no mind to the snakes. He kicked one that rose to bite her and it flipped through the air. Another shook its tail, poised to attack him, but just then Caleb fired at the ground close to his boot and hit the snake instead. The serpent's head exploded in a gory spray.

Elsie was headed straight for a cluster of writhing forms. Her long coat, open at the bottom, exposed her legs. The rattling had risen to a crescendo, the booming of the two revolvers was like thunderclaps. Yet it all fell on deaf ears. Elsie didn't hear, she didn't see.

Fargo ran to Elsie's side and pushed her with his shoulder, attempting to divert her before it was too late. She tripped, recovered, and weaved to the left—toward more rattlers. The men on the crest roared with mirth. They roared louder when a snake struck at her but missed. Fargo kicked it away before it could strike again, then bounded forward to kick dirt at others. There were too many, though. Far, far too many. He couldn't be everywhere at once.

A big snake on a waist-high boulder sensed Elsie's approach and reared its squat head, fangs bared.

"Look out!" Fargo darted over to make it give ground but the reptile was faster. It lashed out, biting Elsie in the thigh. She never cried out, never so much as blinked. She just kept on shuffling, her blank gaze unnerving.

Caleb had stopped firing and was chortling with the rest.

Farther down the slope, Madelyn, Wes, and even Susan were still on their feet. Fargo wanted to help them, too, but there was only so much he could do. The rattler that bit Elsie had slid off and now she was shambling toward four or five others, at the base of the tilted rock. "No! Stop!" he shouted, kicking dirt in a bid to make them slither elsewhere. But he might as well have kicked grass at them.

A sinuous form arched upward. Then another. And a third. Three strikes in as many seconds, all in the same leg. Elsie tottered and slowed but, astoundingly, plodded on.

Fargo had seldom felt so helpless, so intensely frustrated. Thinking of all she had been through only compounded it. She had stood her own against Jacob Sline. After being repeatedly tortured, she hadn't given in. Then Ira Hender had done something to her as well, reducing such a strong, resourceful woman to a vegetable. Fargo could think of only one deed that would account for it. And he vowed to attend to Ira personally.

Elsie's knees were buckling. As she sank onto them, her arms went as limp as wet rags. Her wide eyes were on the sky.

Fargo reached her and bent. "I'm so sorry," he whispered. "But Hender will pay. I swear to you, that slug will pay." Was it his imagination, or did a flicker of a smile curl her mouth? It must have been, because she abruptly exhaled and pitched forward, as lifeless as the rocks and boulders.

Whoops and hollers reverberated in the gulch. Fargo glanced up, and never in his life had he craved to kill anyone as much as he did the men above. But first things first. Whirling, he started down, leaping from bare rock to bare rock, always on the lookout, always alert. The commotion had agitated the snakes, and now most were coiled and rattling madly, ready to strike at any hint of a threat.

Fargo angled to the right, landed on a flat rock, and was set to spring to another when a darkling shape hurtled out of shadow, its curved fangs sliced at his shin. A sharp spin on his part, and the snake cleaved empty air. It began to coil at his very feet but Fargo was on the move again, always jumping, never still for an instant because to stand still was to court the same end as Elsie's.

The rattlers were a veritable legion. There were more than Fargo had ever seen or ever heard of being in any one place at one time. In the middle of the slope they were worst, a writhing sea of serpents with rocks and boulders jutting like islands from a roiled ocean. Many scattered as he landed on nearby rocks, his shadow falling across them. Many more lunged at him. He was constantly dodging, shifting, evading. And without his arms to help for balance, he was always in jeopardy of spilling to the ground, of being engulfed and pierced by a dozen fangs before he could hope to get back up.

Fargo dared not look to see how the others were faring. A single misstep was certain death. He had to concentrate on staying upright and not being bitten to the exclusion of all else. *Leap. Land. Find another safe spot. Leap. Land. Find another safe spot.* Over and over, without end.

Then the snakes thinned out. There were fewer and fewer. Fargo lifted his head just long enough to discover that by some miracle Wes, Susan, and Madelyn had all made it to the bottom. Susan was slumped over in abject terror, Madelyn was gasping for breath. Only the boy stood tall and straight, glaring up the slope at their tormentors.

Another shot rang out and lead sizzled past Fargo's ear. A look upward showed Caleb taking deliberate aim at his back. "Find cover!" Fargo shouted to those below as he zagged to the left. Another twenty feet and he would be with the others, but Caleb was determined to stop him. Three more shots cracked, one brushing his hat.

Fargo vaulted the final ten feet. He landed hard, momentum throwing him onto his knees. For a reason he couldn't fathom, there didn't appear to be any snakes in the lower part of the gulch. He rolled as a bullet spewed dirt by his leg. Coming to rest behind a boulder, he rose into a crouch.

Susan was pressed against another boulder, Madelyn was

flat on her belly beside a third. She had blood on her leg and her dress was torn from the hem to her hip.

"Were you bitten?" Fargo asked.

"No. It's where that rock hit me. It's fairly deep, but I'll survive."

Fargo scrutinized the blonde and the boy. "What about you two?"

"We're fine," Wes said.

"Like hell we are!" Susan declared. "I nearly died a hundred times! My new dress is a mess, and my shoes are all scuffed!"

Fargo wished he knew why the youngster was so devoted to such a shrew. "You're still breathing, which is more than we can say about Elsie."

"Listen!" Madelyn said. "Caleb is yelling' at us."

That he was, his pudgy hands cupped to his pudgy mouth. "—never seen the like! No one's ever made it all the way down before! But now you're stuck there. There's no way out except past the rattlers. And if you're thinkin' of waitin' until dark and sneakin' off, you can forget it. I'm postin' men on both sides. You're boxed in and you'll stay boxed in until you starve or the snakes get you. *Adios!*"

Fargo saw the lawman confer with his eight kinsmen. Four promptly mounted and headed around to the other rim. Caleb then climbed on his horse and trotted off toward Hender's Gap.

Sitting with his back to the boulder, Fargo pondered the situation. They were in a real bind. The gulch was approximately a hundred yards long. At the bottom it was only ten yards across, at the top it widened to some thirty yards. With men on both sides, avoiding sharpshooters would be a challenge. Fortunately, Caleb was content to let heat and hunger finish them off.

"What do we do now?" Wes asked.

It was the first time the boy had ever wanted advice, but there wasn't much Fargo could give. "We can't do anything trussed up like we are." Twisting, he slid his fingers into his right boot and produced the Arkansas toothpick.

Wes grinned. "You're full of tricks, aren't you?"

"A man has to be, to last long out here." Fargo reversed his grip, pressed the blade against the rope, and sawed vigorously.

"I'll remember that when I'm grown up. I'd like to rig it so I can carry a pistol under my arm. No one would ever guess."

"There's more to life than guns," Fargo commented. The position in which he had to hold the knife hurt his wrist, but he grit his teeth and bore the discomfort.

"I just don't want anyone doing to me like they did to a friend of mine, is all," Wes said. "When they gunned him down he was unarmed. No one is ever going to catch me thataway."

Susan was wringing her hands in misery. "Who cares about stuff like that? We need to come up with a way out of this mess."

"Why don't you offer those men up there your body, Susie?" Wes bitterly replied. "Like you did to that hog of a marshal."

"What's gotten into you?" the blonde retorted. "I was doing what I had to. I want to live. Is that so bad? Besides, Wessy, it's your fault I'm trapped here. If you'd left well enough alone, I'd be back in my room at Lily's right now, happy as a lark. I'm sorry you ever came."

"So am I." Wes turned his back to her and slumped against the boulder. "I reckon I have a heap to learn about females and such. I get to thinking one's a butterfly but she's only an old moth."

"Who are you calling old?" Susan said.

Fargo sawed at the rope until he felt the strands start to give. Bunching his shoulder muscles, he exerted all his strength and they gave even more, although not quite enough. He had to saw a little more. It felt great to be able to move his arms. His circulation had been cut off, and now his arms tingled fiercely.

Susan Dixon swiveled, her wrists out. "Do me next! Please! I ache all over!"

"Do you think we don't?" Madelyn said.

The gunmen on the east ridge were seated in the shade of a boulder the size of a log cabin. Those on the west slope couldn't be seen but Fargo had no doubt they were up there, watching and waiting. Flattening, he crawled to Wes and made short work of the boy's bounds. Next he slid to Madelyn.

"Hey!" Susan objected. "What about me?"

"She's hurt. She's before you." Fargo sliced into a loop. Madelyn's features were drawn in agony. When her hands were free, he examined her leg wound. The rock chip had torn through her like a slug, gouging a furrow two inches long, half an inch deep, and a quarter-inch wide. It was still bleeding so Fargo cut a strip from her dress to bandage it.

"Thanks, handsome."

Susan was bouncing on her backside as if she were a ball of yarn. "My turn, my turn! Hurry, please." Her cheeks were smeared with dirt, her golden curls were in disarray, her dress was rumpled, yet she was as lovely as ever, her pouting lips like juicy berries waiting to be tasted.

"Hold still," Fargo said, sinking the toothpick in. The instant the rope fell away, she threw herself at him, mashing her full breasts against his chest and shedding tears of happiness on his neck.

"Thank you, thank you! Now you have to get us out of this frightful fix alive! Please! I'll be eternally grateful!"

To stress her point, Susan kissed Fargo on the ear. Not a light, sisterly peck, but a sloppy, wet kiss, rimming it with her tongue and then swirling the tip of her tongue around and around the hole. Ripples of pleasure prickled his skin as Fargo moved to another boulder that afforded a clear view of both rims. No riflemen had taken up positions. "I'm going to the south end of the gulch. Stay down until I return."

"I'll come along," Susan said.

Fargo had no need of her company but he didn't say so. "Wes, will you keep an eye on Madelyn? She's lost a lot of blood and shouldn't move much."

"Yes, sir."

Another first, Fargo thought, as Wes complied with his orders. Fargo darted to a different boulder, then to another. The rattlesnakes had quieted down, and in the silence he could hear the hammering of his own heart. No outcries were voiced as he warily stalked around a bend and along a straight stretch to another turn. Susan Dixon was glued to his back. When he stopped, she melted against him as if he were bread and she were butter. It made it hard for him to keep his mind on the task he had set for himself.

Doing so became even harder when Fargo came to a cleft that split the west side of the gulch from bottom to top. It was four feet wide at the base, narrowing to a crack on high. Fargo turned sideways, stepped into it, and peered upward to gauge whether it could be climbed. "Keep an eye out," he said.

"I'd rather keep my eyes on you," Susan responded. Sliding in, facing him, she draped her forearms on his shoulders and puckered provocatively. "See anything you like, handsome?"

# 11

Skye Fargo looked at her. Women were fond of complaining that men were only ever interested in one thing, that men were as randy as goats, that most males were all hands and no consideration. But to balance the scales, women had a few quirks of their own, not the least of which was their uncanny knack for picking the most unlikely time and place to give free reign to their passion. Maybe it was because women usually held their carnal hunger in check, and when they finally let it out they didn't much care where they were when the whim struck.

"What's wrong?" Susan Dixon asked. "Why are you staring at me like that?"

"You want me to make love to you *now*?"

"Sure. Give me one good reason why not."

"I can give you three. The men up above. Madelyn and Wes. The rattlesnakes." Fargo was trying to be stern but he could feel the lower half of her luscious body pressed close against his, and despite himself, his manhood stirred. Hell, it did more than stir—it thrust upward like a lodgepole pine.

"Those jaspers up yonder have no idea where we are. Madelyn and Wes can't see us nor hear us. As for the snakes, they're all out in the sun, not here in the shade."

She had valid points but Fargo summed up his feelings by declaring, "It's plain insane, girl. Why now, of all times?"

Susan wriggled to entice him. "Because I'm so wrought

up, I can't stand it. I need to relax. And nothing relaxes me more than this." To demonstrate, she molded her delectable lips to his.

So much for being stern, Fargo mused. Even after all they had been through, even in the godawful heat, her mouth was like watery wine, and as delicious as the real article. She slid her tongue into his mouth and rubbing it around and around, which hardened his pole even more and brought a lump of raw lust to his throat.

When she broke for breath, Susan grinned impishly and said, "There. Still think I'm insane?"

"Yes," Fargo said, much more huskily than he intended.

The blonde pouted like a girl caught with her hand in a cookie jar. "We can make it quick, if that's what's worrying you. Please. I'll be a bundle of nerves all day if you don't help me."

Of all the reasons Fargo had heard, hers was unique. He was tempted. Lord, he was tempted. But he couldn't shake the nagging belief that they were asking for trouble. Evidently she mistook his silence for refusal because she grasped his right wrist, raised his hand, and placed it on her breast.

"Feel for yourself how much I want it."

Her nipple was a rigid nail. Without thinking, Fargo squeezed, and her melon swelled to fill his palm. The lump in his throat grew bigger, and he coughed.

"Surely five minutes can't hurt?" Susan argued. "I won't make any sound. I promise." She kissed his chin, nibbled on his neck, ran her hands up and down his ribs. "See how quiet I can be when I put my mind to it?"

Fargo's blood was boiling, but not from the temperature. He cupped her other breast and she cooed softly and leaned into him, her head tilted, her mouth open and inviting. His own covered it, and the sensation was like sinking into sensual quicksand. She instinctively knew what to do to please a man, her lips and her hands and her grinding hips arousing him to the point where he no longer cared about the gunmen on the crest or Madelyn and the boy or the snakes or anything except the warm, vital body he held and the raw delight she sparked.

"Mmmmmmmm," Susan moaned softly. "Does this mean you've changed your mind, big fella?"

Fargo shut her up with another kiss. Slipping a hand behind her, he explored her back, her buttocks. They were nicely shaped, and satiny smooth. He delved a finger between them as low as he could go and felt the heat her core gave off.

"Ohhhhh, yes, lover, right there, there."

Hiking up her dress, Fargo revealed her exquisite legs. She was flawless, her thighs velvet, her hips responsive to the slightest touch. Another time, another place, and he would dearly love to revel in her beauty, to feast on her charms for hours on end. But he had to be content with a snack.

Susan's fingers traveled to his legs, to his inner thighs, and she stroked him. Her mouth was as fiery as the sun, her tongue a dervish, her breasts cushioning him like twin pillows. Her body was soft in all the right places, complementing his hardness, fusing to him as if their two bodies were one.

A long, deep-throated groan fluttered from her when Fargo drew back enough to cup her down below. Her slit was more than inviting as he inserted his forefinger.

"Oh! Yes!"

Susan bucked against him, her head thrown back, rapture lighting her face. Fargo swirled his finger and felt her inner walls cling to it. He thrust deeper. Susan, gasping, rose onto her toes.

"So good! Do it again! Again!"

Fargo did it many times, adding a second finger and spearing into her with abandon. Their mouths locked and didn't part for long, ecstacy-filled minutes. The whole time, a tiny voice in the back of Fargo's mind warned him to stop, to stay alert, to be on the lookout for enemies, both two-legged and reptilian. But for the life of him he couldn't. He desired to be inside her, to feel her pulsating tunnel enfold his member. And to achieve that goal, he undid his pants just enough for his manhood to poke out.

Susan glanced down. "Land sakes! You're a stallion!"

If so, she was a mare, a mare ripe for mating, and Fargo immediately drew his hand out, dipped a bit at the knees, then lunged up into her as if driving a sword into a sheath. She fit him like a satiny glove.

"Ahhhhhhh!" Susan exhaled. Not loudly, but loud enough to trigger Fargo's tiny warning voice again. "I'm coming already! Do you feel it?"

Yes, Fargo did, and he stood still as she drove herself onto him again and again, impaling herself repeatedly, each time uttering a soft, "Oh! Oh! Oh!" Adrift in a sea of sexual ambrosia, he was content to let time float by. The gunmen could wait, Caleb could wait, Ira Hender could wait. That pesky tiny voice tried to prick him into finishing so he could get on with what had to be done but he hushed it. Everything was just fine, he told himself.

Voices above proved Fargo wrong. He glanced up and saw a shadow flit across the top of the cleft.

"—thought I heard something, Hugh. Let me take a looksee."

Fargo put a hand over Susan's mouth, gripped her waist, and whispered, "Not a sound. They're right over us."

The blonde was slow to respond and Fargo had to pin her against the wall to keep her limbs from moving. A head appeared at the opening, a man with a ruddy complexion and a thick, drooping mustache.

"What's down there?" someone asked him.

"It's too blamed dark to see much," the man with the mustache answered. "Maybe it was a rattler or some other wild critter."

Susan's teeth sank into Fargo's shoulder, her whole body shaking as if she were having a fit. Her fingernails raked his arms.

"Give me a rock, Hugh," the man above said.

Fargo tensed. They had to get out of there, but if they moved they would be seen. A hand came into view, dropping a rock as big as an apple. Fargo lost it amid the shadows, then spotted it falling toward his head. Flinging a hand up, he caught it, a jagged tip digging into his flesh.

The man with the mustache bent an ear toward the bottom. "That's mighty peculiar."

"What is?" his companion said.

"I didn't hear it hit."

"Maybe it got stuck partway down," Hugh said. "What does it matter? No one could climb out of there. The hole ain't big enough."

"I guess you're right," the mustached one said, his head rising, "but it never hurts to be safe."

"Lester, you're a caution. Those four had their wrists tied, remember? Even if they've freed themselves, the only way they'll make it out of the gulch is up either slope. And Clell's bunch and us will be waitin' for 'em."

The men drifted off. Fargo tossed the rock to the ground and licked blood from his palm. He became aware of Susan, still trembling, and of his manhood deep inside of her. "Where were we?"

"Is it safe?" she asked.

"Safe as it can be," was Fargo's response, then had to steady himself when Susan pumped her hips in a frenzy. She had held it in as long as she could. Delirium seized her. Any restraint she had was gone in a puff of her hot breath. She chugged like a Mississippi riverboat, panting heavily, her curls flopping wildly.

Fargo kissed her, kneaded her breasts, her thighs. He sucked on her lips, licked her neck and ear. Her excitement was fast rising to a pinnacle and he wanted to be at the same peak when the deluge came.

"Ohhhhhhh, so fine."

Fargo couldn't agree more. Holding on to her shoulders, he rammed harder and harder, moving faster and faster. She matched his ardor, her legs encircling his waist. The cleft, the gulch, the world seemed to recede into nothingness.

"Ahhh. My stallion! I'm there! Again!!"

That she was. Her climax was shattering and spawned Fargo's own. As she spurted so did he, lancing up into her as if to cleave her in half. It went on and on, his powerful strokes lifting her into the air. Her downward grinding about caved his legs in.

Susan bit him again to stifle an outcry. She quaked uncontrollably, even after they had drained themselves and were coasting to a stop. Even after he sagged against her, totally spent. "See?" she whispered. "I said it would relax you."

Fargo was too relaxed. He didn't hear the scrape of scales on dirt until the source was almost on them. Movement drew his gaze to a rattlesnake as thick as his arm. It had crawled into the cleft and now stopped, sensing them. Its forked tongue darted out. "We have company," he warned, holding tight lest she panic.

"Oh, Lord!" Susan's fear resurfaced and she attempted to pull away.

"Don't, or you'll scare it," Fargo said.

"*I'll* scare *it?*"

The snake started to coil, to rattle. It was so close, human reflexes could never counter its blinding speed. Whichever one of them it attacked was as good as bitten.

Fargo's fingers were iron bands. "Don't speak. Don't twitch." The toothpick, unfortunately, was in its sheath, of no use to him. Nor would moving further into the cleft help. They'd still be within the serpent's lethal reach.

Susan's hips were quaking and the whites of her eyes were showing. The woman was as timid as a rabbit, and like a rabbit her natural inclination was to bolt at the first sign of peril. She pushed against him, in vain. He wasn't about to let her flee. She wouldn't get three feet.

The rattler was coiled now, its tail rattling like a dry

gourd, its unblinking orbs fixed on their legs. The tongue flicked as the head slowly rose, hissing like a lit fuse.

Fargo regretted tossing down Lester's rock. He was ready to leap between the serpent and Dixon, if need be, but he'd prefer it didn't come to that. Flinging his foot back might distract it, allowing him to dive and seize it by the neck. A desperate gambit but he was in a desperate situation.

Susan quivered, earning a hard glance. It was then Fargo noticed she still wore the necklace. Slowly peeling his fingers from her mouth, he moved his hand around her neck. She was puzzled but she wisely didn't ask questions. When he pried at the clasp, her confusion climbed. After it came undone and he began to pull it into his palm, she frowned.

The rattler was swaying like a rope in the wind. Another second or two and it would uncoil faster than the human eye could follow.

Holding the necklace between his thumb and his forefinger, Fargo flipped it at the serpent. Although his accuracy left a lot to be desired, it had the desired effect. The necklace clattered against the wall, and like a flash of lightning the snake struck, its jaws closing on the glittering gold.

The reptile whipped its head violently as if tearing prey apart, the necklace dangling from its mouth. Fargo figured the rattler would let the jewelry fall, but instead, it vanished down the creature's throat.

Susan gave a start. Her arm rose but Fargo closed his own over it, afraid she was going to grab the snake to make it spew out her precious possession. He held fast while the rattlesnake slunk off under a rock.

"Damn you. That was the only one I own."

"Would you rather the thing bit you?" Fargo said in disgust. There was no pleasing some people. Pulling his manhood out, he adjusted his pants and moved from the cleft.

"Where are you going?" Susan quizzed. Rearranging her dress, she followed, casting anxious glances at every rock and crack. When he slowed she collided with him, then clung to his shoulders.

"I don't need a second shadow," Fargo said. "Go sta with the others. Tell them they'll be on their own awhile."

Susan balked. "Go back by myself? With rattlers every where? I'd rather stay with you, lover."

"I wasn't asking you. I was telling you." Fargo had a l to do and couldn't do it with her underfoot. "You'll be saf as long as you avoid the rocks." He kissed her on the chee "I'm counting on you to make Madelyn comfortable an keep the snakes away from her."

"This is a switch. No one has counted on me in a dog age." Susan took a deep breath. "I'll do it. For you. An maybe to prove to myself that I'm good for more than on thing."

Fargo squeezed her arm. "Just be careful."

She nodded and hastened off, slowing after a mere fiv yards to look over a shoulder and gulp. "I'm scared enoug to piddle myself."

"Don't worry. You can do it."

Susan scanned both slopes. "I appreciate the confidenc but I've never been very brave. My pa used to say that whe the good Lord passed out the color yellow, he poured a gal lon down my spine."

Fargo remembered Wes's remarks about her fathe "You'd take the word of a man who lives in a whiskey bot tle? What did your mother think?"

"Ma always called me her bright angel. She said ther wasn't a thing I couldn't do if I put my mind to it." Dixon face softened. "I wish she'd never died. I miss her some thing terrible."

"Then your mother is the one you should listen to," Farg said, his opinion of the blonde rising several notches. "No go. Before someone spots us."

Susan took a few steps, then stopped to smirk and wink "I was serious about repaying you. It'll be a night you' never forget." Giggling, she raced to the bend and was gone

Fargo jogged to the end of the gulch where a steep wall o stone and earth confronted him. A wall much too steep fo

**138**

most men to entertain the notion of scaling it. But most men weren't in his predicament. He searched the ground and found a rock shaped like a crescent moon. It was eight inches long and one end was tapered to a blunt point.

A survey of both ridges confirmed the gunmen were staying out of the sun. Too bad he was denied the same luxury. Leaning down, he dug a couple of footholds with the rock, then straightened and dug more higher up. Jamming the tip of a boot into one, he started his ascent.

It was slow going. A shadow cast by the east slope spared him from the sun for an hour or so, but by noon the sun had risen so high it baked him as badly as it had that day out on the plain when he came across Wes's dead pony. The smart thing to do was to wait for dark, but in the dark, making it to the top would be twice as hard. Then there were Caleb's gunnies. They wouldn't expect anyone to try and make it out of the gulch in broad daylight, and he could catch them off guard.

Provided he lived to reach the top.

Fargo's forehead became slick with sweat that trickled into his eyes, stinging them, making them water and making it hard to see. Every now and then he would stop, dig his fingers into one of the handholds, and wipe his forehead with his other arm. A precarious proposition, for all it would take was one slip and he would plummet to the bottom.

He scoured the top of the gulch often. The four gunmen on the east side were playing cards in the shade of the huge boulder. Those to the west had thrown up a crude lean-to using a blanket. Thanks to the many bends and twists and intervening boulders, odds were they wouldn't spot him.

Tested to their limit, his arms and shoulders ached unbearably. His knees were scraped and beginning to bleed when in due course Fargo saw the rim just six feet away. He reached for a stony knob, levered higher, then resorted to the crescent rock to dig a handhold. Suddenly, out of the corner of an eye, movement registered. Swiveling his neck, he saw Lester and another man who must be Hugh, patrolling the west crest. They were jawing, their rifles slack in their arms. Soon they would come to the end of the gulch and were bound to spy him.

Fargo had maybe thirty seconds in which to act. He stretched as high as he could and gouged out another handhold. It was shallow but it couldn't be helped. His toes bearing most of his weight, he jacked upward, latched on to another jutting stone, and lunged at the rim. His grasping left hand closed on it but the dirt gave way, raining into his face, into his eyes and mouth. Sputtering, blinking, his legs on the verge of slipping out from under him, Fargo clawed for purchase. Taking his life into his hands, he flung his other arm upward.

For a heartbeat Fargo hung by his fingernails. Then he was able to pull himself high enough to thrust both elbows above the rim. He had done it. But he wasn't safe yet. Lester and Hugh were almost there. Flipping up and over, he rolled down a short incline and sought cover behind a low mound of dirt. Not a moment too soon.

"What was that?" The voice was Lester's, he of the droopy mustache.

"What was what?" responded Hugh.

"I heard something."

"You're always hearin' things. It was probably a lizard or a snake. Let's go back. I'm hankerin' for a sip from that water skin."

"Not yet. Whatever I heard, it sounded big."

"Maybe it was a moose. Last I heard, a whole herd of 'em was spotted in the Staked Plain country. One must've strayed this-a-way. I hope we get to shoot it. I've always wanted to taste moose meat."

"Lester, if anyone ever says you have a sense of humor, they're a natural-born liar."

Fargo couldn't see them but he could hear their approaching footsteps. Drawing his right knee to his chest, he gripped the hilt of the Arkansas toothpick. Whether they were Henders or Moselys was irrelevant. They were members of the killer clan and they would gun him down without a qualm.

"Hush, Hugh. What if it's Comanches?"

Moving shadows dappled the mound and darkened over Fargo. The crunch of their boots was like the ponderous tread of a grizzly. Mentally counting to three, he hurled himself erect, prepared to slash and stab.

The two men had their backs to him. They had stopped and were peering into the gulch, Lester with his rifle pointed down, Hugh holding his by the barrel. "See?" the latter said. "Nothin'. Maybe you should have a sawbones check those ears of yours."

"They work just fine. I know I heard something."

Fargo glided up behind Lester and shoved the tip of the toothpick into the small of his back. "It was me. Don't turn around." Both men stiffened and Lester started to swivel anyway, until Fargo pushed on the knife hard enough to make him realize the consequences. "You're a dead man if you or your partner try anything. I want both of you to hand me your rifles. Just ease them back nice and slow."

Hugh was willing to comply but as he began to do so, Lester rasped, "No! I'll be damned if I'll let anyone get the drop on me with a measly knife! We'll both jump him at once. He can't get the two of us."

Fargo couldn't believe what he was hearing. He had a blade pressed into the man's back and Lester didn't care? "Why die for Ira Hender?" he asked to give Lester second thoughts, but it had the opposite effect.

"Why? Because he's my uncle. He gave us an order and I mean to carry it out. So you might as well put down that pig-sticker or one of us will put lead into you."

Hugh wasn't as confident. "Les, I say we do as the man wants if he promises not to hurt us or anyone else."

"You'd believe him?" Lester retorted. "No. We kill him. We kill him now." And with that, Lester sprang to the right and swept his rifle up.

Hugh, a split second later, leaped to the left.

They left Fargo no choice. He had practiced throwing the toothpick so many times that his throw now was mechanical, a swift arc of his arm that sank cold steel into Lester's throat. Spinning, Fargo drove his foot into Hugh's groin while grasping the rifle and wrenching it. It came loose, and Fargo reversed direction, swinging the rifle like a club. The stock bashed against the side of Lester's head, felling him in his tracks. Reversing again, Fargo smashed Hugh on the ear. He didn't intend to knock the man over the edge but that's what happened. Half unconscious, Hugh made no sound.

Lester, though, was wheezing and gurgling and convulsing. He clawed at Fargo but couldn't reach far enough. "You—you—!" he spluttered through lips flecked with reddish spittle.

"Was Ira really worth it?" Fargo asked. He would never get an answer. Lester died in a spreading pool of blood.

The two rifles were an old Sharps and a new Spencer. Fargo picked the Spencer because it held seven shots instead of one. In Lester's pants pocket were extra cartridges. Lester also had a Remington revolver which Fargo wedged under his belt.

The rest was ridiculously easy.

The two cutthroats under the lean-to were dozing. They were taken completely unaware when Fargo snuck up on them. At gunpoint he forced one to bind the other, then he tied the second man after making him remove a store-bought shirt and a broad-brimmed hat. The gunman's build and his own were close enough in appearance that when Fargo donned the shirt and hat, he could pass for the man at a distance.

Four horses were lazing in the heat. Fargo selected a big sorrel and traveled the rim to the other side of the gulch. Two of the four men posted there were sleeping in the shade. The others were still involved in a game of poker, and the dealer looked up and squinted.

"Sheldon? What the hell are you doing on Lester's horse?"

Fargo leveled the Spencer. "I'm not Sheldon."

The dealer cursed and stabbed at a pistol and died as he touched it. The other cardplayer spun into a slug that demolished his face. Both sleepers jumped up and likewise tried to clear leather, but all Fargo had to do was work the Spencer's lever twice.

Just like that, it was over.

Or rather, Fargo reflected, just beginning. He would collect dry brush and make torches, which would keep the rattlers at bay while he brought the women and the boy out. Then it was on to Hender's Gap, alone, to settle accounts with the ruler of the roost. And this time, only one of them would live to walk away.

# 12

Coyotes were abroad both in and out of town.

Skye Fargo listened to their shrill yips as he neared the festering den of iniquity. Gruff laughter came from several points. The Henders and the Moselys were celebrating. Apparently they assumed all their problems had been solved, that things would calm down and life could go on as they were accustomed to. They couldn't be more wrong.

Fargo had left Madelyn, Susan, and Wes in a dry wash in the hills. They had water, they had jerky, they had weapons and enough ammunition to hold off a horde of bandits. He needn't worry about them. But he should be concerned for himself. Here he was, about to brazenly reenter the stronghold of his enemies. Should anyone recognize him, a pack of rabid man-killers would soon be baying at his heels. Which explained why he still wore Sheldon's shirt and hat and was riding the sorrel.

Fargo circled around and entered from the north. A canopy of stars brightened the firmament and there was a light breeze. As he passed the picket fence in front of Lily's Place a man at the gate smiled and waved.

"Did you hear the news, cousin? Ira gave everyone the night off! Fetch a bottle, grab a gal, and frolic until the roosters crow."

Whistling, the man strutted to the porch and tromped on in. Fargo reined to a hitch rail nowhere near a window, and dismounted. From the saloon spilled a blustery clamor, oaths and laughter and tinny music. People strolled the street, happy, content. Couples arm-in-arm, swaggering men who swilled rotgut, ladies in low-cut dresses. Holding the Spencer close to his leg, Fargo turned.

"What's your rush, big man?" A tipsy woman stepped from a doorway, her red dress and her sultry leer marking her as one of Lily's girls.

Fargo smiled and said, "Caleb wants to see me. I'm on my way to the hotel."

"Caleb ain't there, sweetie," the woman informed him. "He's over at the saloon, guzzlin' coffin varnish. I saw him there not five minutes ago." She hooked an arm through his. "What say I take you there? I can use some more gin myself."

To argue would arouse suspicion. Fargo didn't resist as she steered him across the street, babbling like a brook.

"This'll be a night no one will forget. Ira says we're to enjoy ourselves. Drinks are half price. And Lily is havin' a two-for-one night."

Several men lounged in front of the saloon. Fargo thought they were getting some fresh air, but they were outside because they couldn't get in. People were packed like bees in a hive, so many, they were shoulder to shoulder.

"Will you look at this!" his escort said. "How's a girl supposed to quench her thirst? Stick close to me, big man, so we don't get separated." Unfolding her arm, she plowed into the crowd like a mad cow, shouldering and shoving everyone aside.

Fargo stayed where he was, and when she was lost amid the revelers, he turned and crossed to the Hender Hotel. The lobby was deserted. Jonathan was at the desk, buried in his ledger, scribbling. "Why aren't you taking part in the celebration?"

Without lifting his head the bespectacled clerk answered, "Someone has to be on duty at all times. And truth to tell, I'd rather be here than out merrymaking. I'm not much of a drinker or womanizer."

Fargo placed the Spencer on the counter, the muzzle pointed at the man's midsection. "How about Ira? Is he taking part?"

Jonathan looked up, and blanched. "You!"

"Me."

"But Ira announced you were dead! All you troublemakers were disposed of! Those were his exact words."

Fargo nodded at a door at the end of a short hallway. "Is he back there now with his bodyguards? Or did he give them the night off, like everyone else?"

"I won't tell you a thing," Jonathan declared. "You can't make me, either. I might not look very tough, but you can thrash me within an inch of my life and I'll never give in. So do your worst."

Stepping around the counter, Fargo grasped him by the front of his shirt and shoved him toward the hall. "Why bother, when I'll find out soon enough? We'll go together. You lead the way."

"I'm not going anywhere." Jonathan folded his arms. "Ira might believe I've betrayed him, and punish me. I'm more afraid of him than I am of you."

"Is that so?" Fargo rammed the Spencer's stock into the pit of the clerk's stomach and Jonathan snapped forward like a broken stick, sucking air like a blacksmith's bellows. "Next time it will be in the face. Unless you want to gum your food the rest of your life, quit stalling."

Jonathan teetered to the wall and leaned on it. "Why hurt me, mister? I've never done anything to you."

"You're as innocent as a newborn baby, is that it?" Suddenly all of Fargo's anger and frustration boiled over and he gripped the clerk by the throat and slammed him against the wall. "No one in this town has clean hands. Not Sam, not Charley, not you. You help hide the most vicious outlaws in Texas. And when they ride off to kill and steal, the lives they take are on the shoulders of everyone here."

"But all I do is check them into the hotel! I can't be blamed for what they do elsewhere."

The man just didn't see it, and Fargo doubted he ever would. Pushing him, Fargo jammed the Spencer into his ribs. "After you. Keep your hands at your sides. Act as you usually would."

Reluctantly, Jonathan walked to the door and opened it. Another, longer corridor led into the bowels of the building. Licking his lips, he said quietly, "You'll never leave alive if you don't leave now. Ride out while you can. I promise I'll never tell a soul."

Ahead was a second door, partially ajar.

"Why lose your life over a bunch of strangers?" Jonathan wouldn't let up. "What are they to you? Will anyone thank you? Does anyone even care?"

"Shut up."

Light framed the doorway, broken by flitting shadows. Fargo took hold of the back of Jonathan's neck and whispered, "Warn them and you'll never hear the shot that shatters your spine."

"Please. Be sensible."

"Tell that to the family One-Eared John murdered down on the Pecos last winter. Or the old man Vincent Tully shot in San Antonio when the old-timer caught him cheating." Fargo squeezed Jonathan, hard. "Not another damn word."

Through the crack Fargo saw the great slug, as One-Eared John had called him, on the plush divan, being waited on by two young women about Susan Dixon's age. Hender's moon face regarded both lecherously as he sipped at a mug of alcohol. Rum, judging by the bottles on a nearby bar.

As Fargo looked on, a petite girl in a black dress brought Ira a tray containing meats and cheese. Ira grunted like a hog, selected a morsel, and plopped it into his maw. When his thick fingers caressed the girl's cheek, she shivered.

"What's wrong, my dear?" the slug rumbled. "Can't quite get used to my appearance, is that it? You will, though. A month from now you'll think I'm the most handsome man alive. Either that, or your mind will be mush."

Fargo thought of Elsie, and slammed into Jonathan. The clerk was driven into the door and through it, to sprawl on the expensive carpet. Both women jumped and whirled. Ira, though, calmly shifted his bulk, and smiled.

"What have we here? Mr. Fargo, whole and well." The patriarch chortled, his huge mass shaking like pudding. "I must admit, I'm surprised. You're harder to rub out than a cockroach. Am I to gather the men who were left at the gulch won't be returnin'?"

Fargo sidled to the left, past Jonathan, who cringed like a beaten cur. He saw his Henry and gunbelt near the divan, where they had been placed the previous night. "I want you to know something," he said coldly. "At one time or another I've tangled with badmen from the Mississippi to the Pacific, from Mexico to Canada. I've lost track of how many I've had to put lead into. But I've never wanted to shoot anyone as much as I do you."

"I'm flattered." Ira sipped some rum, and belched. "But as you can see, I'm unarmed. And from the stories they tell about you, you're not the kind to shoot a person who can't defend himself. You're not a murderer, Skye Fargo."

Fargo's finger was on the trigger. All he had to do was squeeze and the malignant pile of pus would reap his just reward. But he hesitated. God help him, Hender was right. He wasn't a merciless killer, and never would be. It wasn't in him.

"What are you waiting for?" a newcomer demanded.

In the doorway stood a small figure whose oversized hat had been pushed back, revealing his youthful face. A face in which blazed eyes older than their owner had any right to be. Clasped steady in his small hands was an Eagle Arms pocket pistol taken off one of the dead men at the gulch. He cocked it as he moved toward the divan.

"Wes, no," Fargo said.

The boy had eyes only for Ira Hender. "I came here to kill

the varmint who took Susie away. I reckoned it was Jacob Sline, but he worked for you, mister. So that makes you the hombre I'm going to kill."

Ira guffawed, spilling rum over his shirt. "The brat, too? This is priceless! Next one of the women will waltz in and threaten me."

"No, they're safe up in the hills. I snuck off when they were sleeping." Wes skirted the hotel clerk. "I figured getting this close to the high muck-a-muck would take some doing. But everyone in town is having such a grand time, no one gave me a second look."

"Give it up, boy," Ira said. "You can't kill me any more than your friend can."

Fargo knew better. "Don't do it, Wes. Remember, there's no turning back from a killing."

"I told you once before. When a bug needs squashing, you squash it."

It finally dawned on Ira the boy was serious. Troubled, he lowered the mug and propped himself up on one arm. "Now hold on. I'm no insect. Murder me and you won't be able to live with yourself."

Wes halted, his hands seeming to glow thanks to the nickel-plated revolver, which reflected the light from a lamp. "Liar. You murder folks all the time and you don't appear broken up about it."

Ira set down the mug and sat up. "Listen, boy. You say this is about your cousin. She's alive, isn't she? No one did anything to her she didn't want done. And she likes it in Hender's Gap, as I recollect. So why hold a silly grudge?"

"Susie is kin."

"Ah. That I can understand. Family is everything. All I do, I do for mine. You'd make a fine Hender or Mosely. In fact, why don't you stay with us? Susie can go back to Lily's and you can work over to the general store with Sam. Your own job, five dollars a week, and all the hard candy you can suck on? How'd that be?"

Fargo slanted toward Wes. Now it was Ira who didn't see

the truth facing him, who didn't realize John Wesley might look like a boy and talk like a boy but he was no child to be bribed with sweets.

"We can adopt you into our clan," Ira said, "you and your cousin, both. Maybe set you up in a little place all your own. Think of it. No more parents to boss you around. No one tellin' you when you should go to bed, what you should eat, when you can and can't play. It would be every boy's dream come true."

Fargo stopped. Wes had lowered the pistol and appeared to be considering Hender's offer.

"I'd never see my ma or pa again? Never hear my pa quote Scripture or have to listen to my ma carping about how clean my room is?"

"Exactly." Ira beamed in the assurance he had the youngster wrapped around his finger. "Your life would be yours to live as you see fit."

"That's mighty kind of you, to do all that for me," Wes said, and he beamed, too. "The only problem is, I love my folks. My pa wearies me with his Bible-thumping at times. And Ma makes me eat greens when I don't want to. But they're family, just like Susie is family, and we never turn our backs on our own kin." The pistol rose again. "I reckon that's all that needs saying."

Ira's moon face contorted in fury. "Enough of this nonsense. Jonathan, kill them both, and be quick about it."

Fargo had taken his eyes off the hotel clerk. Now he pivoted and saw Jonathan on his knees, unlimbering a pair of Whitney pocket pistols. The mouse had fangs. From the speed with which Jonathan drew and the proficiency he showed in cocking both revolvers as they swept up and out, he knew how to use them. The Spencer boomed first, rocking Jonathan. But the clerk was as tough as he had boasted and didn't go down.

Lead and smoke erupted from the Whitneys as Fargo darted to the right. Jonathan missed, but not by much. Instantly, Fargo levered off two swift shots that smashed into the clerk's chest.

Jonathan was punched backward. Snarling like a panther, he righted himself and thumbed back the hammers once more.

Fargo heard another shot. Wes had fired, but he couldn't look to see if what he feared most had occurred. He blasted another round into Jonathan Hender, which should have been enough to end the gunfight. But, amazingly, the clerk stayed on his knees and fired again, his shots missing by a whisker, only because Fargo was still in motion, still moving to the right.

Working the lever, Fargo wedged the stock to his shoulder and sighted down the barrel. He needed to finish it, needed to finish it now and stop Wes from making the biggest mistake of his young life. If it wasn't already too late.

"Damn you!" Jonathan screeched, elevating the Whitneys.

This time the Spencer's slug rocked the clerk's head from front to back, drilling through the center of his forehead and exploding from his skull. In pure reflex Jonathan triggered off two more shots but they plowed into the floor instead of into Fargo.

There were still three rounds in the Spencer. Fargo rotated, hoping he was wrong, that Wes hadn't shot Ira Hender. But the boy had.

Up on the divan, the lord of Hender's Gap pressed a hand to a bleeding wound on his shoulder and gaped in astonishment at John Wesley, who was slowly advancing. "You did it! You actually shot me! I didn't think you had it in you!"

"I reckon a lot of people will make that mistake," Wes said. "If you know any prayers, say them while you still can."

Fargo sprang toward the boy but stopped when the revolver was trained on him. The gleam in Wes's eyes left no doubt what he would do if pushed. "You'd shoot me, too?

After all we've been through?" Fargo questioned the young hellion.

"I came all this way on account of him. I mean to buck him out in gore and I won't let anyone stand in my way."

Beyond the boy, Ira Hender was sliding toward the Henry and Colt. His rotund body oozed like a great glob of grease, his bloody hand outstretched. He was grinning, thinking they didn't notice, that triumph was in his grasp.

Fargo had the Spencer close to his hip, the barrel tilted upward. As Wes began to swivel toward the divan, he took a hasty bead. Ira grabbed the Henry, pointing it at them at the very moment the Spencer boomed.

"No!" Wes cried. "He's mine!"

Ira Hender was no one's, now. A third eye had blossomed between the others. Frozen in place, as rigid as a board except for his slack mouth, he stood there another five seconds, then keeled forward. The impact reminded Fargo of the time he'd seen a redwood chopped down. It resounded throughout the hotel, causing furniture in the chamber to bounce.

"He was mine," the boy repeated softly.

Fargo discovered the women were missing. Had they gone for help, he wondered, or run off? A shout in the distance galvanized him into dropping the Spencer and sprinting to where the Henry lay. Then he leaped onto the platform and traded the Remington for his own Colt and gunbelt.

Wes hadn't moved, and was staring glumly at the great hulk on the floor.

"We're not done yet," Fargo told him. "The whole clan will be up in arms."

"Let them come," Wes said. "The first one to show up, dies."

"We can't beat all of them," Fargo reasoned. "But we can see to it that Hender's Gap is as dead as its founder."

Wes perked up. "Kill a town? Now that would be something."

Fargo had never met anyone so young so fond of dealing death. The boy worried him. He truly did.

"How do we go about doing it?"

"Grab a couple of lamps." More shouts from elsewhere in the hotel were incentive for Fargo to hurry to the nearest table. Holding a lamp by the base, he hurled it at the divan. The glass globe shattered and flames spurted, spreading like wildfire.

Wes laughed and threw one at a sofa that combusted into a blazing pyre in seconds. "I get it!" he cried, going to another lamp on an oak stand. "We'll burn this place down around their ears!"

The rear door opened. Fargo had heard the latch being raised and turned as Hiram and his beanpole friend rushed in. Both were so jolted by the sight of their slain patriarch that they halted just inside. Fargo whipped the Henry up, saying, "Drop your rifles!"

"Go to hell!" Hiram replied.

Whatever else could be said about the Henders and the Moselys, they died game. Fargo shot each once but neither would fall. Hiram zinged a slug past his head, the beanpole sent one into the ceiling. Fargo quickly fired again, before Wes could join in, hitting each man in the sternum. That was that.

Flames were crackling across the carpet toward the walls. Smoke swirled in growing tendrils that would soon form into a cloud. Within minutes the whole chamber would be consumed, and once it was, there would be no extinguishing the fire. From the hotel it would leap from building to building, sealing the destruction of Hender's Gap.

"Let's go!" Fargo yelled, dashing for the back door. Jumping over Hiram, he stopped so the boy could catch up. But Wes wasn't coming. The youngster had grabbed another lamp and flung it at the curtains. "That's enough!"

Wes's face glowed. Not from the fire, but in savage glee at the wreck and ruin he was helping to create.

"Now!" Fargo insisted. The hue and cry would have the

town's population down on their heads in no time. When the boy dawdled, watching flames eat the curtains, Fargo sped over and gripped him by the arm.

From the hallway in front spilled a cluster of men. Waves of flame checked their rush, but some spotted Fargo and the boy and opened fire.

Ducking, Fargo yanked Wes down beside him and barreled into the night. He bore to the right, passing alley after alley. Only until they had gone far enough would he deem it safe to head for the street. Once there, they'd take their pick of any horse they wanted and be gone before a hunt was organized.

"Let's set more buildings on fire," Wes suggested.

"One is enough," Fargo said. There wasn't enough water in the whole town to save the hotel, let alone the other structures that would soon be aflame.

Bedlam ruled. Men and women scurried in confusion and panic, the women bawling or screaming, the men shouting questions and curses. In the midst of the mayhem, no one noticed Fargo or his charge. He pulled the boy toward a hitch rail, slowing when he saw the Hender Hotel.

The blaze was spectacular. Sheets of fire licked skyward from most windows. Columns of smoke reared like gray tornadoes. Already, flames had jumped to adjacent shacks and their roofs were roaring cauldrons.

Fargo hastened on. He had to sidestep a terrified woman who flew by, shrieking. Four horses were tied to the rail, all of them skittish. "Take the bay," he directed Wes, and moved toward a palomino. Grasping the reins, he hiked a boot to the stirrups just as the boy cried a warning.

"Mr. Fargo! Behind you!"

Fargo spun. It was Caleb. The lawman was ten feet away and had him dead to rights. Both Smith & Wessons had been drawn, the hammers were back, Caleb's pudgy fingers were wrapped around the triggers. The lawman smirked, relishing the moment.

That was when a pistol cracked, a single shot barely heard

above the pandemonium except by those close to the hitch rail.

Caleb Hender recoiled as if slapped, his brow knitting as a red rivulet trickled from a neat hole above his heart. The Smith & Wesson sagged, as did Caleb, his mouth working soundlessly.

Fargo stepped past the palomino. Gunsmoke rose from the end of the boy's pocket pistol. Wes had just slain another human being but he was as calm as if it were only target practice.

"My first lawman."

People were taking cover, bellowing, bawling. Fargo threw the youngster onto the bay and forked the palomino. No one tried to stop them as they wheeled and galloped out of town, and once Fargo was convinced there was no pursuit, he headed westward toward the hills. Hender's Gap was a seething inferno, a raging fiery tempest, half the structures afire and more igniting every minute. Its inhabitants were pouring into the high grass in a steady stream. A handful had formed a bucket brigade, but they might as well try to stem a buffalo stampede by waving sticks.

Madelyn and Susan were anxiously waiting, seated on a rise. When Fargo and Wes arrived, the blonde bounded to her feet and hugged her cousin close. "You did it, Wessy! You made them pay for how they treated us!"

"Now can we go home?" the boy asked. "Things will be different. I'll have a talk with your pa. From here on out, he'll treat you right. I promise."

Until well past midnight they watched the spectacular show, the women gleeful, Wes somber, Fargo tired and thankful the ordeal was over. He turned in before they did and was up earliest. A survey of the valley failed to turn up a living creature. From what he could see, Hender's Gap was deserted. During the night a mass exodus had taken place.

Two hours later Fargo drew rein at the edge of the charred remains of the once thriving community. Not a single building still stood. Blackened husks were all that was left of one man's monument to his own greed and lust for power.

"I reckon this is where we part company," Susan said. "Wessy and I are heading home." Leaning toward Fargo, she whispered, "I'd sure like to show you how grateful I am. But I need to get him home safe. You understand, don't you?"

Yes, Fargo surely did. The women embraced, and he shook the youngster's hand. "Remember what I told you. Living by the gun will put you in an early grave."

"I suppose. But I'd rather breathe dirt than eat crow."

What could Fargo say? He didn't ride on until the two Texans were dots in the distance, and as he reined the Ovaro around, he commented, "There's one boy that would make any parent old before their time."

"Wesley's not his last name, you know," Madelyn said.

"It isn't?"

"No. I don't know where you got the idea it was. Susan told me last night his real name is—" Madelyn tapped her temple. "Darn. I can't rightly remember. It was Hardesty or Hardlin or Hardin, or something like that." She shrugged. "Not that it matters much. He'll grow up and grow out of his orneriness. Most do."

Fargo hoped so. If not, one day Wes would leave a trail of bodies from one end of Texas to the other. Clucking to the stallion, Fargo thought about Santa Fe, and the long trail there with Madelyn for company, and he smiled as he rode into the brilliant sunshine of a brand-new day.

**LOOKING FORWARD!**
The following is the opening
section from the next novel in the exciting
*Trailsman* series from Signet:

**THE TRAILSMAN #215
DUET FOR SIX-GUNS**

*Colorado, 1860, where casinos sprang up to cater to
the grifters and drifters, ranchers and rangers,
cattlemen and cowpokes, bumpkins and bankers.
They offered every king of amusement but too often
served death and deceit. . . .*

The big man on the magnificent Ovaro let a smile of appreci-
ation touch his lips as he drew in the full, rich beauty of the
land. This was fertile, fecund terrain where the lower Colorado
River nestled between the San Juan and Sangre de Cristo
ranges of the Rocky Mountains. Towering stands of cottonwoods, blackjack oak, red cedar, and aspen mingled with wide
open rolling fields. Vast banks of fireweed, their vibrant pink
spires shimmering in the sun, edged equally wide carpets of
Rocky Mountain iris, their blue-violet leaves infused with purple veins. In the distance, a bed of delicate yellow brittlebush
formed a striking contrast of shape, texture, and color.

But suddenly the big man's lake blue eyes narrowed and
turned cold as an ice floe. His lips thinned and anger knotted his
stomach. When beauty was marred, loveliness defaced, anger
always stabbed at him. It could be an ugly stain on a lovely garment, a shattered hole in a beautiful vase, a delicate painting
ruined by a jagged tear, a fine horse with a badly swollen, neglected hock. It didn't make much difference what. It was
beauty defaced, splendor marred, loveliness destroyed that af-

fronted him, and now it had happened again, unexpectedly. But it was always unexpected, he reminded himself. This time it was black-winged, ugly forms slowly circling through the sky that defaced the beauty of the scene. He watched their almost motionless flight and knew them for what they were—symbols of death, messengers of decay.

Skye Fargo moved the Ovaro forward, his eyes following the slow, downward spiral of the huge, black wings just beyond a small shrub-covered rise. Pushing his way through a stand of tall vervain, he crested the rise, his frown deepening, as he saw two figures on the ground, both young women, both lying on their backs. A half-dozen buzzards walked across their lifeless bodies. Powerful, hooked beaks at the end of red-skinned heads tore skin strips of flesh from the two still forms. Fargo drew his Colt when he suddenly saw he was not alone at the grisly scene. *Goddamn,* he cursed silently. Two horsemen emerged from a line of red cedars across from him, both wearing only breech-cloths and armbands. He immediately backed the pinto down the rise until he was out of sight behind the vervain. He watched the two horsemen approach the figures of the two young women, swinging from their ponies with smooth, lithe movements. The buzzards reluctantly took wing as the two men stepped to the bodies.

Fargo's eyes fastened on the armband of the one of the Indians, seeing the distinctive beadwork design. "Wind River Shoshone," he muttered as the Indian bent down to one of the young women. He curled a hand around long, blond hair and pulled her head up. He drew a hunting knife from the thin, rawhide waistband of his breechcloth and started to bring the knife down to the woman's head. "Look good hanging on teepee pole," the Indian said to his companion. Fargo knew the Shoshone language well enough to understand. Drawing the Colt, Fargo started to bring it up, but then dropped it back into the holster. The two Shoshone might have friends nearby, he reminded himself. As the Indian pressed the edge of the knife against the young woman's scalp, Fargo spurred the Ovaro forward over the rise.

"No, you don't, you two-handed vulture," Fargo bit out, seeing the Shoshone drop his hold on the girl's hair as he spun. But the pinto was charging at full speed and as the Shoshone raised the knife to strike, he had to quickly duck away as the horse bolted toward him. Fargo leaned from the saddle, brought the Colt out and down in a sweeping blow that grazed the Shoshone's head. The Indian pitched forward, and sprawled facedown on the ground. He shuddered, then tried to lift himself up but Fargo had already leaped from the saddle, landing only a foot from the Indian. This time, the Colt crashed down on the man's head with full force. The Indian collapsed and lay still. As Fargo whirled, the second Shoshone charged at him, a tomahawk raised in one hand. The Indian brought the short-handled ax down in a furious chopping blow that Fargo easily ducked, then ducked away again as the Indian attempted a flat, sideways blow. Fargo shifted his hold on the Colt, his fingers closing around the barrel to leave the heavy butt free.

Once again, the Indian swiped viciously at him with a short, quick chop of the ax that Fargo barely avoided. The Shoshone, a slender but tightly muscled figure, shot two more blows at him with his war ax as Fargo tried to strike at the man's head with his Colt. He had to drop low to avoid the Indian's catlike reaction, the tomahawk grazing his scalp as the Shoshone struck out once again. Fargo narrowly avoided the tomahawk's sharp edge realizing the Shoshone was extremely fast with his weapon. Circling, Fargo feinted and saw the Indian move with him, ready to strike a counterblow at his first chance. Fargo started to move in, swinging wildly with the Colt. The Indian easily avoided the blows, striking out with his own counterblows in quicker, more accurate responses. Fargo saw the Shoshone wait in a half crouch, confident that it was but a matter of time before his strokes hit their mark.

He waited for Fargo to come at him again. Fargo obliged, feinting left, then right, and the Shoshone responded, bringing the tomahawk down in quick, vicious arcs. Fargo made another feint and the Indian struck back at once. But this time Fargo didn't try to reach the man's head. Instead, he brought the butt of the Colt down on the Shoshone's wrist as the man swung the ax down in another counterblow. He heard the man gasp out in pain as the butt of the Colt smashed into his wrist, hitting bone, tendon, and nerve. The tomahawk dropped from the man's hand as Fargo brought the Colt around in an upward arc, smashing it into the Indian's jaw. The Shoshone staggered backward, his jaw suddenly hanging open at a grisly angle. Fargo swung the Colt with all his strength, and the Shoshone's forehead split down the center with a rush of scarlet.

The brave fell in a heap on the spot and lay still. Fargo straightened, drew a deep breath, and turned the Colt in his hand as he strode to the two young women on the ground. Kneeling, he examined their dresses, finding only empty pockets with nothing to identify either young woman. As his eyes moved across both of their bodies, a furrow dug into his brow. The wrists of both young women bore circular bruise marks. They had plainly been bound. Then, amid the scars from the vultures, he saw the round holes in each of the young women's breasts. It wasn't hard to put it all together. They had been trussed up and held prisoner, but had managed to escape, only to be caught and killed and left for the buzzards.

Fargo's lake blue eyes again turned to ice as they lingered a moment longer on the two young women. Both were reasonably young, probably once attractive before the buzzards had descended upon them. "Rest their souls," he muttered, cursing silently. He had nothing in his saddlebag with which to dig, but he took a moment to gather enough loose stones and broken branches to cover both young women's torn bodies. Finishing, he climbed onto the Ovaro and rode away, grateful for small victories, if only over a flock of vultures. He rode with his lips still pulled back in distaste, anxious to leave the spoiled and broken beauty, heading the pinto east across streams filled with leaping rainbow trout. The sun still bathed the high peaks of the Sangre de Cristo Mountains when he came to a wide road. He followed it through a long valley until a town finally came into view.

He slowed as he drew closer to the town, seeing that it had taken on new dimensions. At the time of his last visit, years back, Bearsville had been a ragged place. Now it exuded an air of solidity with new buildings along the wide main street, a bank, an expanded general store, a barbershop, and a town meeting hall. He saw the usual freight wagons, Owensboro mountain wagons, and top-bowed Texas wagons, but he also noted a sprinkling of phaetons and surreys. Cowhands, prospectors with their tool-laden mules, along with well-dressed gentlemen, walked the wide street. He was surprised only at how quickly Bearsville had sprung up. It was a town in a good place for growth. Men with money from Denver, Colorado Springs, and Canon City could easily visit from the north, as could money from Santa Fe and Albuquerque in New Mexico, to the south, not to mention all the newly prosperous miners and businessmen in between.

Fargo slowed as he came abreast of a large two-story building with bare-breasted maidens carved alongside the entrance doors. Gold letters marched across the top of the entranceway. BEARSVILLE EMPORIUM, he read and, in slightly smaller letters: GIRLS AND GAMBLING, FUN AND CULTURE. Fargo rode on as he noted that the second story of the building was circled with small windows. He'd gone on another few streets when he drew to a halt in front of a window sign that bore the word *sheriff*. His hand pressed the letter in his pocket, a reflex gesture. Hank Carlson had sent it and Hank didn't ask for help lightly. Fargo had agreed to visit as soon as he'd finished breaking trail for the Cole brothers in Kansas. Besides, he hadn't seen Hank in years. It was time for a reunion. Hank Carlson was a good sheriff when he was back in east Kansas, an honest and fair man. He was just as good a one in Colorado, Fargo was certain.

Dropping the Ovaro's reins over the hitching post, Fargo stepped into the sheriff's office. Two men immediately turned to him as he entered. It took him a long moment to recognize the one that rose. The Sheriff Hank Carlson he'd known had dark red hair, a ruddy complexion, full cheeks, and a strong face. The man before him was a study in gray, his face thin, cheeks sunken, hair wintry gray, skin the gray of old dust. Fargo tried not to let the shock show on his face and knew he'd not really succeeded as Hank Carlson came toward him. "Fargo, you made it. God, it's good to see you," the sheriff said, and Fargo grasped a hand that had only half the strength he once knew.

"Got your letter. Came as soon as I could, Hank," Fargo said.

The man nodded and Fargo saw a sadness come into his face. "I'm not the man you knew, old friend, but you can see that," the sheriff said. "I'm sick, real sick." He turned to the other man. "This is Doc Berenson. He spends a lot of time with me, gives me enough pills to keep me doing my job as best I can," Hank Carlson said.

"I do whatever I can," the doctor said, rising, a tall, thin-faced man, balding with a narrow nose, steady eyes with a quiet competence to him. "Glad you could make it, Fargo. Hank's been counting off each day waiting for you." The sheriff turned away as Doc Berenson met Fargo's eyes, giving a helpless shrug that said volumes. Hank Carlson's voice broke Fargo's grimness.

"I'll be turning in my badge soon enough, Fargo," the man siad.

"Got somebody to take it, Hank?" Fargo asked.

"An old acquaintance, Sam Walker. But he can't do it for another month, maybe two. There are a few things I have to take care of before that. One of them is sitting in the next room in a cell," the sheriff said. Gesturing for Fargo to follow him, they crossed to an adjoining room, which was a six-by-eight-foot cell. A man sat on the edge of a narrow cot, a stringy figure with a foxlike face and small, darting eyes. "Freddie Steamer. He's a very special prisoner," the sheriff said. "He and his gang have made a career robbing over a dozen banks from Idaho to Iowa."

"He's the only one you caught?" Fargo questioned.

"We got lucky. He came here to visit a girlfriend and we got him, been holding him ever since. His girlfriend pays him an occasional visit. I let her. I keep hoping she'll let something slip," Hank Carlson said. "I did learn that his gang is watching the town. That's why I called you. I'm supposed to deliver him to a federal judge in Oklahoma."

"But you're not well enough to do it," Fargo guessed.

"That's only part of it. The other part is his gang is waiting and watching. Seems he's the only one who knows exactly where all their stolen money is hidden. I need someone to break a new trail out of here with him. I need you, Fargo," Hank Carlson said.

"Don't see where it'd be all that hard," Fargo said.

"It will be. There are places that give you cover every way out of Bearsville. His boys are at each of them, you can be sure. You're the only one who might break a trail past them. Will you do it for me, Fargo?" Hank Carlson asked.

"I'm here. Got nothing better to do," Fargo replied. Carlson offered a grateful smile as Fargo followed him from the room. The sheriff sank heavily into a chair behind the desk and Doc Berenson took Fargo aside.

"Thanks. That's better medicine than any I can give him," the doctor said.

"How long does he have?" Fargo asked, his voice hardly a whisper.

"Can't say for sure, except not long," the doc said and Fargo swore silently as he went on to the front office. The sheriff rose as he came in, opened a desk drawer, and pulled out a star-shaped tin badge. He leaned forward and pinned it onto Fargo's shirt.

"No deputy's badge, not for you, Fargo," Hank Carlson said. "This town can stand two sheriffs, if only for a little while." He nodded toward the adjoining cell room. "When do you want to take him?" he asked.

"Tomorrow morning. I need a good night's sleep," Fargo said.

"I've extra rooms at my office," Doc Berenson offered.

"That'd be fine." Fargo nodded. "How many in Steamer's gang?" he asked Hank.

"Eight, but I'd guess they've hired some extra eyes," Hank said. "Remember, it's only after you've gone a ways out of town that they'll be watching. I don't know how you can get him through by day."

"Maybe I can't. I'll decide that in time," Fargo said when the door opened and a young girl entered, perhaps eighteen, Fargo guessed. A tight blouse made more of modest breasts than they deserved and Fargo took in her curvy, swinging hips. Her youthful face was attractive in a sullen, pouty way. Brown hair hung loose and long, and she carried a basket in one hand.

"Cooked some things for him," she announced belligerently,

her eyes fastening on Hank Carlson. Fargo knew who she was at once. The sheriff took the basket from her, examined the contents, and handed it back to her. She raised her arms as he patted her down, searching for the bulge of a six-gun or derringer. "Enjoy yourself?" she tossed at him defiantly when he finished.

"Watch your mouth, girl," Carlson growled. "Go on in." The girl hurried into the adjoining room, giving her hips an extra obstinate sway. "Lola Carezza," Carlson said to Fargo.

"She just his girlfriend or part of his gang?" Fargo queried.

"Wish I knew. I'd arrest her if I had anything to charge her with," Hank said, lighting a lamp as night descended. "I'm running out of energy. That doesn't take long these days. But I'll have Steamer ready for you come morning."

He reached into the desk drawer, brought out an envelope and handed it to Fargo. "Official transfer papers for Steamer. For Judge Frederick Bolstrom, in Oklahoma City. Don't take Steamer lightly, Fargo. He knows there's a hangman's noose waiting for him when you deliver him to Judge Bolstrom."

"I never take desperate men lightly," Fargo said. "See you in the morning."

"Thanks again, old friend," Hank said.

"Glad to help," Fargo replied and followed Doc Berenson outside and down the street to a neat, white-painted building that bore the single word *clinic*. A small barn behind the building let him stable the Ovaro and Fargo was shown to a room that was one of three in a row, all identical, each spare and neat, with a freshly made up hospital bed. He undressed in the moonlight from the window and stretched out on the bed, finding it firm but comfortable.

The visit hadn't been what he'd expected, a reunion that was bittersweet, at best. Yet he was not unhappy that he had come. It was a good feeling to do a favor for an old friend in bad times. The thought stayed, comforting him during a night of less than sound sleep. When morning came, he rose, washed and dressed, and went outside to saddle the Ovaro. He had just finished when Doc Berenson came up to him. "I'll come back after I've delivered Steamer. Hope you can keep Hank going," Fargo said.

"I'll try. No promises, I'm afraid," the doctor said. Fargo

walked the short distance to the sheriff's office. A faded brown gelding stood tied to the hitching post.

"In here," Hank Carlson called out and Fargo followed his voice into the adjoining cell room. Freddie Steamer sat with his hands tied behind his back. Hank Carlson holding a rifle on him. Steamer wore a high-crowned Stetson pushed back on his head. "He's all yours, Fargo," the sheriff said.

"Untie him," Fargo said as Hank Carlson's eyes grew wide.

"Untie him?" the sheriff frowned.

"I saw too many Indian pony prints on the way here. The Shoshone may give me more trouble than his friends. I want him able to stop quick when I tell him, and run if we have to. He'll need his hands to handle his horse. I don't want to lose my scalp along with his," Fargo said.

"Whatever you say," Hank said with faint disapproval as he untied Steamer's bonds. The man rubbed his wrists and Fargo noted the crafty smirk that flashed in his beady eyes.

"Outside," Fargo commanded and walked the man to the brown gelding. He watched Steamer swing onto the horse. The man's eyes cut to Fargo as he pulled himself onto the Ovaro.

"Not keeping your gun on me?" Steamer asked, sarcasm edging his voice.

Fargo smiled pleasantly. "No need to," he said.

"You think you're that fast?" Steamer sneered.

Fargo kept the smile on his face but his hand moved with the smoothness and speed of a diamondback's strike. The Colt fired the instant it cleared the holster and Freddie Steamer's hat blew from his head, a neat hole almost magically appearing in the crown. Steamer's mouth dropped open. "That answer you?" Fargo said softly. Steamer said nothing, but he swallowed hard. "Pick up your hat," Fargo ordered and the man swung from the gelding, retrieved his hat and returned to the saddle. "Ride," Fargo said, keeping a half pace behind the gelding.

He steered the Ovaro through town, casting a curious glance at the Bearsville Emporium as they passed. Two men were plastering signs on the outside of the building. One read: FAMOUS OPERA SINGER PERFORMS. COME LISTEN. Another read: CULTURE IN COLORADO. He half smiled as he rode from town, starting down the road into the wide valley. His eyes swept the thick forest that rose on both sides, mostly red cedar and hackberry with clusters of cottonwoods mingling with the open land in the center of the valley. Turning, he moved into the red cedar forest, staying among the trees as he slowly rode forward with his prisoner. Steamer rode quietly, nary a word from him, but Fargo didn't let the man's silence lull him into relaxing. Steamer was a desperate man who'd spend every minute looking for a chance to run. But he wouldn't take any wild risks, Fargo was certain. The hole in his hat was a reminder he'd not quickly forget.

Fargo peered into the trees, his eyes sweeping across the land, pausing at every slope and rise, looking for any movement of leaves or brush that was made not by nature but by man, alert to the subtle differences only a trailsman or an Indian scout would note. With each broad search he brought his eyes back to Steamer, taking in the way the man sat his horse, the tension in his posture, the deliberate set of his shoulders and hands. But he saw nothing to make him suspect Steamer was preparing to make a break for freedom. Instead, the man looked faintly uncomfortable, leaning forward in the saddle. Fargo returned to searching the distant trees and his next glance at Steamer show the man looking more uncomfortable, both his hands now tightly gripping the saddle horn. Steamer lifted his eyes to look at Fargo and his lips pulled back in a grimace. "Got to stop," he breathed. "My stomach. It's killin' me."

"Your girlfriend's cooking?" Fargo asked wryly.

"Didn't eat anything else," Steamer said and groaned. "Let me off the damn horse . . . just for a few minutes."

They had been moving over uneven terrain, Fargo admitted, and nodded at Steamer's request. "Get off," he grunted, watching the man slide from the saddle and sink to the ground, bending over with his arms pressed to his stomach. "Don't do anything stupid," Fargo warned.

"I'm too busy hurtin'," Steamer muttered.

Fargo watched the man stay stooped over, both arms pressed against his midsection, his foxlike face drawn tight. Fargo didn't see anything tricky in the man's actions. On his knees, arms held to his stomach, Steamer was in no position to try and run or make any quick moves. Fargo took his eyes from the man and peered through the trees again, once more searching along the distant line of forests. He brought a quick glance back to Steamer and found the man had straightened up some, but was still on his knees. "Ready to ride?" Fargo asked.

"Just a few minutes more," Steamer said.

Fargo brought his gaze back to another sweep of the open land and the clusters of red cedar when, out of the corner of his eye, he caught the sudden movement of Steamer's arm. Snapping his gaze back to the man, he was just in time to see Steamer pulling the knife from inside his shirt. "Damn," Fargo bit out as Steamer flung the blade, a narrow, double-edged stiletto. The man's throw was fast and entirely too accurate as Fargo saw the knife hurtling at his stomach. Pressing on the stirrups, he pushed himself upward, lifting his body as he twisted away from the stiletto to try and take the blade someplace less fatal than his gut. Still clinging to the saddle, he knew he had managed to avoid the sharp, narrow knife plunging into his vitals as he felt the impact of the blade. A flash of gratefulness swept through him as he felt no sharp, sudden pain.

He yanked at the Colt to pull it from the holster, but the gun refused to come out. Glancing down at his side, he saw the hilt of the stiletto protruding from the holster. In a freak, ten-thousand-to-one chance, the stiletto had gone through the opening of the trigger guard of the revolver, deep into the other side of the holster where it was now imbedded. It became a barrier that wouldn't let him pull the Colt out of the holster, and he gave up trying after another two attempts to free the weapon. The sound of hoofbeats echoed through the air and he saw Freddie Steamer racing off on the brown gelding.

"Son of a bitch," Fargo growled as he sent the Ovaro into a gallop, seeing Steamer heading for the edge of the tree line to race into the open. At a light slap against his powerful, jet black neck, the Ovaro put his powerfully muscled hindquarters into play and, skirting trees, he closed ground quickly before Steamer's faded brown gelding could reach the forest's edge. The man turned the horse away and tried escaping through the trees, but found the Ovaro quickly cutting him off again.

Steamer tried to turn, racing back behind Fargo to reach the tree line, but Fargo sent the pinto into a tight spin, coming abreast of the fleeing prisoner as open land rose up only a hundred feet away. He brought the Ovaro alongside the brown gelding, one arm raised to take the blow he expected Steamer would throw. But the man surprised him, flattening himself in the saddle and clinging to the horse now only a dozen yards from the open land.

Rising up in the stirrups once again, Fargo flung himself in a sideways dive and landed atop Steamer. Gripping onto the man, he fell from the horse with him, hitting the ground hard and hearing Steamer's breath fly from him. Rolling aside, Fargo pushed to his feet and looked at Freddie Steamer who lay face-down, gasping for breath. He allowed the man another half-minute to recover the wind that had been knocked from him, and as Steamer started to regain his feet, Fargo slammed him against the trunk of a big red cedar. With a groan, Steamer slid down to his knees against the tree. Fargo stepped to the Ovaro, taking the lariat from its saddle strap.

Using the blade of the Arkansas toothpick from his calf-holster, he cut a length of the lariat and tied Steamer's hands in front of him. "Guess we'll do it Hank's way," Fargo muttered. The gelding had halted at the edge of the trees and Fargo brought the horse back, then pulled Steamer to his feet and pushed the man onto the gelding. Draping Steamer's hands atop the saddle horn, Fargo stepped back and reached one hand down to his holster, where his fingers curled around the smooth hilt of the stiletto. He had to yank hard before the blade came free of his holster. When it emerged, he turned the weapon in his fingers and saw how the narrow flatness could have been carried in by Lola without being detected, probably hidden in the waistband of her skirt. "She smuggle this to you yesterday?" Fargo asked Steamer.

"No," Steamer said sullenly. "I've been keeping it to use at the right time."

"Almost the right time," Fargo corrected, swinging onto the Ovaro and leading the way forward, shrouded by the tree cover again. He hadn't gone more than ten minutes more when he pulled to a halt. A sound filled the forest, a sound that seemed to make everything stop.